Surprise
Endings

Surprise Endings

ROBIN JONES GUNN

BETHANY HOUSE PUBLISHERS
MINNEAPOLIS, MINNESOTA 55438

Surprise Endings
Revised edition 1998
Copyright © 1991, 1998
Robin Jones Gunn

Edited by Janet Kobobel
Cover illustration and design by Lookout Design Group

A Focus on the Family book published by
Bethany House Publishers
A Ministry of Bethany Fellowship International
11400 Hampshire Avenue South
Minneapolis, Minnesota 55438
www.bethanyhouse.com

Printed in the United States of America by
Bethany Press International, Minneapolis, Minnesota 55438

Library of Congress Cataloging-in-Publication Data

Gunn, Robin Jones, 1955–
    Surprise endings / Robin Jones Gunn.
        p. cm. — (The Christy Miller series)
    Summary: Fifteen-year-old Christy hopes to make the cheerleading squad,
but she faces a jealous classmate, financial constraints, and complications with
two guys she's interested in.
    ISBN 1–56179–600–X (pbk.)
    [1. Cheerleading—Fiction. 2. Christian life—Fiction.] I. Title.
PZ7.G972Su   1991
[Fic]—dc20   91–43
                                           CIP
                                         AC

99 00 01 02 03 04 05 / 15 14 13 12 11 10 9 8 7 6 5 4 3 2

To my parents,

Travis and Barbara Jones,

who encouraged me to be
only what God made me to be—
nothing more, and certainly nothing less.

Contents

1. Dreams for a Price 1
2. Rah-Rah Girls Don't Quit 13
3. Hopeful Romantics 21
4. Under the Flower Trellis 29
5. An Enchanted Evening 41
6. Inside, Outside 51
7. Jasmine and Other Poisonous Flowers 61
8. Prom Plans 75
9. Jealous Love 89
10. A Hollow Victory 101
11. I Can Wait 115
12. A Laurel Crown 129
13. Surprise! 139

CHAPTER ONE

Dreams for a Price

Oh yeah! We've got the spirit
Oh yeah! That cougar spirit
Say, hey! Get outta our way
Cougars are on the prowl TODAY!

Christy Miller ended the cheer with a long, leggy leap. The other girls watched her land just slightly off balance.

"Good, but try to keep your arms straighter next time," the cheerleading adviser said.

Christy nodded at Mrs. James and tried to not feel self-conscious, even though so many girls were standing around watching her.

"And be sure you stretch out after practice today." Mrs. James turned her attention to the next girl in line.

Stepping away from the critical stares of the varsity cheerleaders, Christy took a deep breath and silently mouthed the cheer. Keeping her arms straight, she began going through the motions again.

It seemed to Christy that the first few days of practice hadn't been very hard or very competitive. Now that it was getting closer to tryouts, there were fewer girls showing up every day. And the ones who did show up were, in Christy's opinion, all much better at jumps than she'd ever be.

"Give it a rest, Miller!" one of the varsity girls said, coming in her direction. It was Renee, a junior with short, dark hair and eyes like a raven's.

Christy tried to ignore Renee and finished the cheer with a solid jump.

"Give it up. You're not cheerleader material, and you know it. Besides, you're only a sophomore."

"Sophomores can try out like anyone else," Christy said quietly, lifting her damp, nutmeg brown hair off the nape of her neck. She shaded her blue-green eyes from the afternoon sun and tilted her head. "Tryouts are only two weeks away, Renee. And I'm not going to drop out."

Christy meant the statement to sound firm and threatening, but it affected Renee as much as a harmless kitten batting at a thread.

"You only made it this far because of Rick Doyle." Renee flung the words at Christy. Two of her friends now stood beside her. "So don't look so innocent. We know what's going on between you and Rick."

"Between me and Rick?" Christy couldn't stand the way the three girls were staring at her. She wasn't sure what Renee was trying to prove. "Rick and I are just friends."

"Oh, right. Friends. Buddies," Renee said sarcastically. "That explains why the most popular guy in school hangs out with a little sophomore who thinks she's going to be next year's star cheerleader."

Christy felt her heart pounding and her throat swelling. *Why is Renee all over me like this?*

"Come on, Renee," said one of the other girls who walked over toward Christy. "Leave her alone. It's not Christy's fault Rick turned you down."

Renee spun around. "Who asked for your opinion, Teresa?"

"It's Teri. Only my grandmother calls me Teresa. 'Teresa Angelina Raquel Moreno,' " Teri mimicked in a high-pitched voice with a heavy Spanish accent. "But you're not my grandmother, Renee. So you can call me Teri, like the rest of my friends."

Christy admired Teri's friendly spunk. She obviously wasn't threatened by Renee. Christy wished she could appear as confident as Teri. But then, Teri was a junior, like Renee, so that had to count for something.

Renee turned to glare at Christy with a hard, pinched expression. "You're not good enough, Miller. Okay? You're not good enough to be a cheerleader, and you're definitely not good enough for Rick Doyle." Renee turned with a flashy cheerleading swish and marched off the field with her two friends beside her.

"What was that all about?" Christy asked Teri. Her hands were shaking. "What did I ever do to her?"

"It's not you," Teri said, wrapping her long, wavy, brown hair up in a knot and trying to secure it with a scrunchie. "She's mad at Rick and she's just taking it out on you. Don't let her get to you. You're doing great, Christy. By the time tryouts get here, you'll be ready. Don't worry."

But Christy did worry. She worried all the way home. As soon as she was in the front door, the first thing she did was call her closest friend, Katie, to tell her about the incident.

"Oh come on, Christy," Katie said in her bubbly, self-assured voice. "You know what Renee's problem is. It's Rick. She likes Rick. Didn't you know that? Everybody knows that."

"Katie, almost all the girls at Kelley High like Rick. He and I are good friends, you know that."

"Sure I do. But Renee doesn't. She thinks he's taking you to the prom."

"The prom? Why in the world would she think that? My parents would never let me go to the prom. You know how strict they are."

"Well, get this. I heard that Renee asked Rick to the prom, and he turned her down."

"You're kidding! Why?"

"That's what she's so upset about. He didn't give her a reason, but from what she heard from one of his friends, Renee thought he was taking you."

"No way! He'd never ask me. He could choose from a dozen girls, all seniors. Besides, I think a senior guy should take a senior girl. I mean, it's their last year of high school and everything."

"Christy, get a clue! He wants to take you. The problem is, he thinks you won't go with him, since you're not supposed to date until you're 16."

Christy twisted the phone cord around her finger and said, "But Katie, I'm the kind of girl Rick teases and calls when he's bored. I'm not the popular rah-rah type that he'd take to the prom. He's probably waiting to find out who's got the best chance of winning prom queen. That's who he's going to take."

"Wake up, girl! Don't you see what's happening? Rick is turning you into the rah-rah, prom-queen type. You're like putty in his hands. He's making you into the perfect girlfriend."

"Katie, that has to be the most ridiculous thing you've ever said!"

"Ridiculous or not, it's the truth."

A frustrating silence hung between them.

"Christy, I didn't mean to hurt your feelings," Katie said, all the fire doused from her voice. "But if you don't think I'm right, then just ask yourself to honestly answer one question." Katie paused.

"Yes?" Christy knew that although Katie often went overboard with her exuberance, she also could be right sometimes.

"Ask yourself, 'Would I have tried out for cheerleader if Rick hadn't talked me into it and gone with me to practice the first day?' "

"Yes," Christy answered immediately. "I would've gone on my own."

"Don't answer me. Answer yourself. Honestly. And if you're honest, I think you'll see what I'm saying. Rick has more control in your life than you realize."

For at least 20 minutes after they hung up, Christy remained sitting on the hallway floor, with her back against one wall and her stocking feet against the other, searching her heart for an honest answer to Katie's question.

The tricky part was, Christy had always wanted to be a cheerleader. She had thought about it a lot when tryouts were announced. But maybe Katie had a point. Deep down, Christy wasn't sure if she ever would have worked up the nerve to try out if Rick hadn't coaxed her into going to the first practice.

However, Christy quickly reasoned, Todd had a lot to do with it, too. If Katie wanted to talk about Todd's influence on Christy, well, that was another story. She would gladly admit that Todd had a unique way of challenging her and of directing her decisions. He had since the day they met on the beach last summer. She remembered looking up into the screaming silver-blue eyes of this tall, blond surfer and thinking how he fit her description of the perfect guy. Then she got to know him, and Todd became an important part of Christy's life. He strongly influenced her when it came to things that mattered in her heart.

Even though Todd lived two hours away, when it came right down to it, if she had to define their relationship, she would consider Todd much closer to one day being her boyfriend than Rick. Christy and Todd saw each other only a couple of times a month, but Todd was in her heart. Forever. Nothing could ever change that. And what mattered to Todd mattered deeply to Christy.

She tugged at her socks, cuffing them and uncuffing them, remembering when she had scrunched in the hallway last week, the night before the first cheerleading practice and talked on the phone with Todd for an hour. Christy had told him all about how she was thinking of going out for cheerleader and eagerly waited for his opinion and encouragement.

But all Todd had said was "I think if you're going to do it, you should do it for the Lord."

"You mean I should pray about it?" Christy had asked.

"That's part of it. But you need to think about how you can take some risks on your campus. If you become a cheerleader, you'll have an audience."

"An audience?"

"There will be lots of people who suddenly know who you are, and they'll watch your life a lot more closely. You can't just blend in with the crowd anymore. Being a cheerleader might put you in a good position to let people know who you really are and what your life is all about."

"I hadn't thought about that."

"Being up front can be good. It kind of forces you to take a stand for what you believe."

Christy had taken Todd's words to heart, and that night she had written in her diary:

God, I want to do this cheerleading thing for You. I know Todd's right. If I become a cheerleader, people will look up to me and respect me. That will give me a better chance to tell them that I'm a Christian and maybe to invite them to church with me or something. I just want whatever is best, and I want to be a good example to others.

In thinking through the whole situation now, Christy felt certain that even if Rick hadn't walked her to practice that first day, she still would have gone. Her heart was set on doing this, and just as Todd had advised, she would do it for all the right reasons.

"Christy," her mom called from the kitchen, "are you off the phone yet? Dinner is ready. You need to come set the table."

"Coming!" Christy left her cheerleading thoughts huddled in the hallway as she went into the kitchen. Her mom had made stew, which wasn't her favorite dinner. Mom's "stew" generally consisted of whatever leftovers had been in the refrigerator long enough to be unappealing if eaten by themselves. They were all dumped into the Crock-Pot in the morning and left to simmer all day until they became "stew."

Venturing a sniff of the concoction, Christy had to admit it smelled good. She teased her mom, saying, "Spices are your friends, aren't they?"

"What?"

"You know how to put in just the right seasonings to make even leftovers smell as though you started fresh."

Mom gave Christy a puzzled look.

"Never mind," Christy said. She realized what she was saying was not exactly a compliment and would be better left unexplained.

Her mother stepped in to make a familiar point. "We need to be thankful we have food on the table, Christy. It may not be fancy, but we've never gone hungry, and we should be grateful for that."

"I know," Christy said quietly. She pulled the silverware from the drawer and began setting four places at the kitchen table. The last thing she wanted to be reminded of tonight was how tight money had been since her family moved to California from Wisconsin. Or how all of them needed to work harder to stay on their budget.

At dinner, Christy's nine-year-old brother, David, monopolized the conversation. Christy and her mom and dad all listened patiently as David reenacted, with considerable exaggeration, his teacher's facial expression when she found gum on her shoe.

He was kind of funny, for a little brother. But Christy would never tell him that. It would only encourage his goofiness.

As soon as David excused himself from the table, Mom leaned over, and a sweet smile spread over her lips. Christy knew that look. Her mother was trying to create an encouraging environment. Christy also knew her mother was about to say something Christy probably wouldn't be glad to hear.

"Dad and I have gone over the paper you brought home from the cheerleading adviser, and we've decided that the only way for this to work is if you find a way to come up with half of the money."

"Half!" Christy squawked. "That's more than $300!"

"Well," Dad said slowly in his deep, authoritative voice, "is this something you want to do? Are you willing to commit yourself to the practices and the games?"

"Yes." Christy tried hard to hold back the tears that pressed against the corners of her eyelids.

"Your mother and I think it's a worthwhile goal. It's also a big commitment," Dad said. "And an expensive one. We feel you should share a part of that responsibility by participating in the financial responsibility."

Christy wanted to say, "But you don't understand! There's more to this than me fulfilling my goal. Can't you see that? This is something I need to do so I can take a stand on my campus." But as usual, Christy couldn't make the really powerful words come out, and all she said was "How am I going to come up with that much money?"

"You have to understand, Christy, that this expense isn't in our budget. But we're willing to find a way for it to work out for you, if you're willing to come up with your half. You could baby-sit this summer," Mom suggested.

"Get a position during the weekdays with someone who has small children. Perhaps you could advertise in the toddler Sunday school class you've been helping out with the last few weeks. You could let some of the parents know you're available."

"Baby-sit? This summer?" Christy decided this wasn't a good time to mention to her parents that she had been planning to stay in Newport Beach all summer with Uncle Bob and Aunt Marti, just like last summer. Christy already had a long list of plans for things she and Todd were going to do. She hadn't even considered the possibility of staying home in Escondido all summer—especially to baby-sit.

"You decide how you want to come up with the money, Christy," Dad said. "If you're serious about doing the cheerleading, we're with you 100 percent, and we'll find a way to come up with half the cost. But you've got to put in your share, too. It's time you learned there are no free rides."

"I definitely want to do it. I mean, I want to at least try out and see what happens," Christy said.

Mom sat back in her chair. "Before you give such a firm

answer, why don't you think about it some more. In the mean-
time, do you have much homework tonight?"

"Tons."

"I'll do the dishes, then," her mom said. "You can do them
tomorrow night. You'd better get at your homework."

In the sanctuary of her room, Christy found it impossible to
concentrate on her "tons" of homework. She went over to her
dresser and picked up the San Francisco music box her aunt had
bought her on their trip there last summer.

Winding the brass key on the bottom, Christy set it back on
the dresser and watched the ceramic cable car move up the little
hill as it played "I Left My Heart in San Francisco."

*Wish I knew where I left my heart. It certainly doesn't seem to be
where it's supposed to be tonight,* Christy thought. *I feel pulled in so
many directions.*

She was convinced that becoming a cheerleader ranked as an
important dream at this point in her life. It was a worthy goal.
Weren't adults always telling her to set goals? She believed being
a cheerleader would be something she could always look back on
and say, "I did it! I worked hard, and I accomplished my goal."
Plus, she would be able to take a stand for what she believed, as
Todd had said.

But she never dreamed she would have to come up with half
the money. And baby-sitting all summer to come up with the
money was practically the last thing Christy wanted to do with
her precious free time.

It seemed there were so many obstacles to her trying out for
cheerleading. The incident with Renee had been discouraging
enough. Now she had the money part of it to struggle with, too.
She never guessed it would be so hard.

Do I want to be a cheerleader badly enough to really work for it? With a determined twist of the knob, Christy wound up the music box once more. Effortlessly, the little cable car took its free ride to the top of the glassy hill.

CHAPTER TWO

Rah-Rah Girls Don't Quit

Decision-making had never been Christy's strong point, and she knew it. For three days now, she had wavered on whether to try out for cheerleader. Her legs ached from all the jumps at practice, and Renee had continued to take every opportunity to remind her that she was "lower" than the rest of the group.

Every day Christy told herself it wasn't worth it and she should skip practice. Yet every day she went, halfheartedly hanging in there, anxious for a good enough reason to stay, willing to accept a respectable reason to give up.

At lunch on Thursday she looked for Rick. He had been a great encouragement when he walked her to practice that first day. Then he'd done one of his famous disappearing acts and ignored Christy. Or maybe he was avoiding her. Whatever it was, she decided it was time to get his opinion.

When she found him clustered with his usual batch of senior friends, Christy boldly approached the group. Rick spotted her, smiled, and called out, "Hey, Rah-Rah!"

Christy gave him a look she hoped communicated he was embarrassing her and she wanted him to leave the group to talk to her. Rick read her expression amazingly well and stepped away from the group.

"Don't tell me," he said, towering over Christy, warming her with his chocolate brown eyes and teasing her with his half smile. "You flunked your algebra quiz."

"No," Christy said softly, "the quiz is tomorrow. It's something else."

"It's your parents, right? They want to move to Romania because housing is cheaper."

Christy let out a puff of a laugh. "No, Rick. It's something I'm trying to decide."

Swarms of students passed them on both sides, making it a noisy, confusing spot to carry on a conversation.

"Well, the answer is red."

"What?"

"If you're trying to decide what your best color is, it's red. You look great in red."

Christy stared up at him without responding. *This is pointless. Why did I think he would be serious long enough to offer any help in this situation?*

"Never mind," she said and started to walk away.

Just then the bell rang.

"Wait a minute!" Rick said, catching up to her and grabbing her by the elbow.

Christy looked at him, but she couldn't decide what to say. She wasn't mad at him, just confused; and his joking had made her dilemma seem trivial. She tried to think of a way to phrase her question: *Rick, do you really, truly think I should try out for cheerleader?* It sounded stupid and phony. She couldn't think of how to rephrase it so that it sounded like a real problem.

"I'll meet you here after school," Rick said solidly. "Okay?"

He let go of her arm and waited for an answer.

"It's really nothing."

"Just be here," Rick said, walking backward and pointing to the spot where they had been standing. "After school." Then he turned and sprinted toward the science building.

Christy turned abruptly. She ran into a guy who was heading for the garbage can with a handful of trash.

"Whoa, look out!" he said.

Too late. A carton of fruit punch splattered across Christy's arm, staining her white T-shirt with a huge red splotch.

"Sorry," the guy said, then hurried on.

Christy felt like crying when she realized she'd have to go to the rest room to clean herself up, and then she'd be late for class. As if things weren't bad enough, Christy heard Renee's snippy voice behind her saying, "It's your color, Christy. You look great in red."

Christy turned to face Renee, but Renee kept walking, her back to Christy, as if she hadn't said anything.

The tears came, hot and fast, streaming down Christy's cheeks. *That's it! That does it! I can't take any more of Renee. I'm not going to try out. Not now, not ever. Never! It's not worth it.*

That was exactly what she decided she'd tell Rick, too. He wouldn't have to help her make a decision because she'd just made it once and for all.

Christy's blazing emotions stayed red hot until after school. With her jaw set, her walk brisk, Christy plowed through the maze of picnic tables ready to give Rick the news. He stood there, waiting for her—cool, tall, confident, oblivious to all the turmoil Christy had suffered that afternoon.

"How's my favorite Rah-Rah?" he called out.

"I am not a Rah-Rah, and I wish you wouldn't call me that!"

"You're going to be." Rick smoothed back his wavy, brown hair and shifted his books to his other arm. "Legs like yours, you can't miss."

Christy gave him her best disgusted look and slugged him in the arm. Rick started to laugh.

"What's so funny?" she asked defensively.

"You. You crack me up!"

That was it! With as much determination in her steps as she had when she first approached Rick, Christy bolted in the opposite direction.

"Wait a minute. Stop!" Rick hollered, coming after her.

Christy didn't stop.

Rick did. He stood still and said loudly and firmly, "I thought we weren't playing this game anymore. You know, the one where you run away and I chase after you."

Christy stopped, but she didn't turn around.

"Come here," Rick said, coming alongside her and pulling her over to a low brick wall. Rick put his books down, took Christy's books and put them down, then waited for her to sit down on the wall.

Rick sat next to her and in a deep voice said, "Now, will you tell me what's going on?"

"It's nothing. Really." She felt so immature. *Why am I so emotional about all this? Why did I start to run away from him again like that?*

"Christy, come on! Don't you remember how weird things were between us after Christmas vacation?"

Christy nodded.

"And remember that long talk we had? The one where we decided 'no more games'? That's what you said. 'No more hiding and running away.' So what's going on?" Rick folded his arms across his broad chest.

Christy looked down, blinking to hold back the tears. "I'm sorry, Rick. It's this whole cheerleader thing . . ."

"And . . ." Rick prodded.

"Renee's right. I'm not cheerleader material. I'm not going to try out."

"Yeah you are," Rick said firmly.

Christy didn't look up. "Even if I made it, my parents say I'll have to come up with half the money. How am I going to do that?"

"You'll find a way."

"It's not worth it."

"Yes it is."

They sat silently for a minute while Christy blinked back a runaway tear.

Rick's voice turned smooth and persuasive. "If there's one thing I know about you, Christy Miller, you're not a quitter. You're better than any of those girls, and you know it. You can't let Renee get to you; she's trying to make you mad enough to quit. Don't let her. You have to give it your best shot. You have to try. Promise me you'll try."

Christy looked up, clear-eyed, her mouth easing into a promising smile. "All right, Rick. I'll try."

"Oh, man!" Rick said, shaking his head at Christy. "If you only knew how you did that!"

"Did what?"

"It's your eyes. You have killer eyes, Christy. You have this way of looking at a guy with those killer eyes of yours, and you don't have any idea what you do to him."

Christy felt the blood rushing up her neck and racing to her cheeks. Then, with a little more boldness than she usually had with Rick, she said softly, "Well, you have a way of using just the right words and making a girl feel like Play-Doh."

"Like Play-Doh?"

"You know. All soft and mushy."

"Well, Killer-Eyes, that's exactly what you do to a guy when you give him that innocence-and-bliss look."

Christy playfully batted her eyelashes and in a Scarlett O'Hara voice said, "You mean like this, Rick?"

"Nope." Rick's expression remained serious. "That's what makes it a killer. You don't even know how you do it. It's just you. It's your innocence. Not many girls at this school still have that."

They looked at each other, and Christy felt warmed, energetic, and more encouraged than she had in days.

"You'd better get going," Rick said. "You're going to be late for practice."

"Thanks, Rick," Christy said, impulsively swinging her arm around his neck and giving him a buddy hug. Rick looped his arm around her shoulders and returned the gesture.

Christy spotted Renee a few feet away, glaring at them. So Christy purposely kept holding on to Rick even after he began to let go.

Rick then put both his arms around Christy and, just to be funny, acted as though he were going to tip her off the wall. But he held on to her and pulled her back up. They both laughed, and Christy noticed out of the corner of her eye that Renee was gone.

At practice, Christy gave it all she had, her enthusiasm making up for her lack of experience. Every time she glanced at Renee, she received flaming, snarly glares. Christy thought if their adviser hadn't been there, Renee might have charged Christy and scratched out her eyes.

It didn't matter. She was going to give it her best shot. She wasn't a quitter. She had made her decision, and there was no turning back now.

CHAPTER THREE

Hopeful Romantics

Christy could barely read her two chapters of history home-work. Her mind was flooded with cheerleader thoughts. Mentally, she ran through all the moves of the routine she planned to do for tryouts next Friday. She pictured herself in the blue and gold skirt and sweater the school had promised to all the girls who tried out. The adviser said all the girls should be dressed the same so the judges wouldn't be influenced by appearances.

Christy put down her history book and cleared a space on her bedroom floor. Facing the mirror on her closet door, she quietly went through the routine, making sure her smile was its biggest and brightest.

She had told herself a dozen times before, and now coached herself again, to give it her best. What she lacked in coordination, she could make up for with enthusiasm. After all, she had killer eyes, right?

With one hand on her hip and the other arm jutting up into the air, her fist tight, Christy froze her position before the mirror and critically examined her eyes, her smile, her stance. She liked what she saw. Taking one more vibrant leap into the air, she imag-ined she was jumping for the judges.

"Christy?" Mom tapped on the bedroom door, then opened it slowly. "Are you still bouncing around? It's after 10:00, and your father is already asleep."

"Sorry," Christy said softly.

"Did you finish your homework?"

"Not exactly."

"Christy, you've had plenty of time to do it. I don't like the way this cheerleading is taking you away from your studies. If your grades suffer, you'll not be allowed to go out for cheerleader. Do you understand?"

"Yes."

"All right, then. Get ready for bed, and I'll wake you up when Dad leaves for the dairy in the morning. You can finish your homework then."

Being awakened at 5:30 in the morning to read history should be some kind of punishment for criminals, Christy decided the next morning. She could barely keep her eyes open at the kitchen table. The textbook lay beside her bowl of cereal like a dried-up, old mummy.

"History is so boring," she moaned to her mom, who poured a cup of coffee and joined her.

"It wasn't to the people who lived it," Mom said.

"Why do we have to study it now? What does it matter?"

Mom's round face looked fully awake, and Christy thought it must be from all the years they had lived on the farm and her mom got up before dawn. She was definitely a morning person.

"The thing about history," Mom said, "is that we should try to learn from people's choices, good and bad. Then we as a nation and as a people should try to make better choices, based on what we know."

"Huh?"

"I don't think you're awake yet, are you, Christy?"

With a huge yawn, she said, "I want to go back to bed."

"Why don't you shower and get dressed? Then you'll be more alert. Have you done all your algebra?"

"Almost."

"I'm serious, Christy, when I say that your grades mustn't suffer because of this cheerleader business."

"I know, I know. I'm going to take a shower. Is my red sweater clean?"

"Your red sweater? It's going to be warm like yesterday," Mom predicted. "It'll be too hot for a sweater."

Christy rose and ambled from the table. "Do I have anything else that's red?"

"Why?"

"Oh, never mind. I'll find something to wear."

It took 20 minutes, but Christy finally decided on a dress she hadn't worn in a long time. It was a summery, cotton dress that badly needed ironing after being scrunched up in the closet for so long.

If her mom proved right, and it was another warm May day, Christy thought she would look fresh and stylish, like the rich girls at her school. They seldom wore the same thing twice and had a variety of accessories to match everything in their wardrobes.

Christy pulled her hair back and worked at brushing her teeth an extra long time. With a wide, cheesy grin in the mirror, she examined her work and thought her teeth looked pretty good. Her hair looked pretty good today, too.

Amazing! How often does this happen? she thought.

"Christy?" called Mom from the hallway.

Christy was working to apply mascara on her bottom lashes

without leaving skid marks.

"You need to leave in about five minutes."

"Five minutes!" Christy jammed the mascara wand back into its holder. "I didn't finish my homework!"

"What have you been doing all this time?"

"I took a shower and did my hair, and then I had to iron my dress . . ." She opened the bathroom door, displaying the finished product.

"Goodness!" Mom exclaimed. "You look as though you're going to church or something."

Just then the phone rang, and David answered it. Christy could hear him say, "Hey, dude! When are you going to take me skateboarding again? Huh? Yeah, she's still here."

Christy dashed to the phone. She knew it had to be Todd. Snatching the receiver away from David, her voice came out as light and pretty as she felt. "Good morning!"

"Hey, how's it going?" Todd's easygoing voice made her feel as it always did: full of anticipation for when she would see him again.

"Do you have to work this weekend?" Christy asked.

"Tomorrow I do. I thought I'd come down to see you tonight, if that's okay with you and your family."

"Of course! You know you're always welcome. What time do you think you'll get here? I'm sure you can have dinner with us."

"Five-thirty okay?"

"Sure."

"Cool. I'll see you then. Later."

"Bye, Todd. Have a wonderful day!"

But Todd had already hung up. He always hung up first. And Christy would always hold the phone, listening to the dial tone, letting her imagination fill in the blanks, since Todd's phone conversations were usually short and to the point.

Christy's parents adored Todd. Her brother idolized him. Once when Todd had come down on a Saturday, he had spent several hours skateboarding with David and then had helped Dad paint the living room. After dinner when he started to wash dishes, Christy had picked up a dish towel and joined him, realizing this might be the only time she would get to spend alone with him.

That's when she realized that with Todd, there would probably never be such a thing as the two of them "going out." Their time together would be with her family and with their friends, and it would be just as much fun as if the two of them went somewhere alone. It felt so natural to Christy that she was amazed when one of her friends at school had said she and her boyfriend had been going out for three months and he hadn't met her parents yet.

"Mom," Christy called out, "Todd is coming for dinner tonight, all right?"

"He is? What time?"

"Five-thirty. Is that okay?"

"All right!" shouted David. "Is he bringing his skateboard?"

"I didn't ask him, but David, don't beg him to spend all his time with you when he gets here, okay?"

David smirked and marched past Christy, snatching his lunch sack off the table.

"Mom?" Christy groaned. "Would you tell David not to bug Todd like he always does?"

"I do not!"

"Yes you do!"

"All right, that's enough." Mom stepped between them. "You're both going to be late for school."

"Mom?" Christy asked, oblivious to her need to get going. "I was wondering something." She paused. "I was wondering if, well, do you think Dad would let me go to the prom with Todd, I mean, if he asked me? Since this is his senior year and everything."

"Oh, Christy! How can you ask me something like that when you're supposed to be walking out the door?"

"Do you think Dad might make an exception if it was Todd?"

"I'm not going to even try to answer that. We'll have to talk about it. Now get going, both of you!"

During first-period history, Christy thought about going to the prom with Todd. Getting a new dress. Having her hair done. It made her feel like Cinderella.

The more she thought about it, the more it seemed like a practical dream—one that needed to come true. After all, this was Todd's senior year, and she was about the closest thing he had ever had to a girlfriend.

She laid her right arm across her open history book and moved her wrist back and forth slightly. Her gold ID bracelet caught little slivers of light, shimmering with promise. Christy ran her finger over the engraved word "Forever." She had felt it many, many times since Todd had given it to her last New Year's Eve, and she knew its touch by heart.

You don't realize how good you have it, Christy told herself. She had Rick as a good buddy at school and church. And she had Todd. She would always have Todd. She just knew it.

We have to go to the prom! It's one of those "forever" memories that a couple like us should have, she thought.

The bell rang, and history was over, with an assignment of two more chapters to read over the weekend. Christy grabbed her books and hurried to meet Katie at her locker, their usual meeting place.

"Cute outfit!" Katie said, her bright green eyes scanning Christy's outfit. "What's the big occasion?"

"Katie, do I look like a girl who is about to be asked to the prom?"

"Oh, I get it. You figure if you look the part, your fairy godmother will be able to spot you in the vast sea of us hopeful romantics, all wishing to be asked to the prom," Katie said with a dramatic twist of her wrist in the air and a swish of her copper-colored hair. "She'll pick you out of the lot of us and make your wish come true, because you look as though you deserve it."

Christy laughed quietly and looked around, hoping nobody had seen Katie's performance. "A girl can dream, can't she?"

"What about the minor detail of your parents?"

"That's the part I'm being extra hopeful about. I asked my mom this morning, and she didn't exactly say no. I mean, I know he would have to ask me first, but I told her since it's his senior year and everything—"

The shrill bell interrupted Christy, so she finished with "It doesn't hurt to set high goals, now does it?"

Katie laughed and bubbled with her usual enthusiasm. "Wouldn't that be great! If your mom didn't say no, then she's probably getting ready to say yes. That's how my parents are. I'm sure your mom will say yes. And when she does, I'll ask Lance to go with me."

Christy looked at her friend wide-eyed. "Do you think he'd go with you? What am I saying? Of course Lance would go with you. Do it, Katie! Ask him!"

"First you find out if you're going," Katie said.

The halls began to clear.

"Yikes!" Katie squeaked. "We're going to be late! I'll call you after school. I hope you do great on the algebra quiz!"

Oh no! I forgot all about the quiz! Christy thought in a panic.

All during her next class, Christy crammed for algebra. But it was no use. Her mind was too full of prom dreams to let anything else in. The quiz was impossible, and she knew she missed at least half the problems.

Christy tried to ignore the sour feeling in her stomach as she recalled her mom saying, "Your grades mustn't suffer because of this cheerleader business!"

CHAPTER FOUR

Under the Flower Trellis

"Next Friday," Mrs. James, the cheerleading adviser, said, "you need to be here right after school to dress for tryouts. Tryouts will be in the gym beginning at 3:30. Any questions?"

"Yes." Renee stepped close to Christy and mumbled under her breath, "What do we have to do to keep Christy from coming?"

"What was that?" Mrs. James asked.

"Oh, I just was saying how fast tryouts are coming," Renee said.

Christy clenched her teeth and swallowed hard. This daily harassment was eating a hole inside her. *What have I ever done to you, Renee? Why are you so mean to me? It's not fair, and I won't let you treat me like this any longer!*

Christy determined that she would beat Renee in the tryouts. She would show Renee and the others that she had the strength and ability to beat them all. It was the only way she could think of that would allow her to get back at Renee.

The girls ran through the routines with mechanical precision, and Christy gave it all she had. By next Friday she would be cheerleader material, and she would prove to Renee that she deserved to be on the squad.

Christy began to take on the same determination about the prom. She would find a way to talk her dad into letting her go. If she tried hard enough, she could find a way—she just knew it.

That anticipation and determination made Christy feel more excited than usual about seeing Todd that night. Her heart brimmed with expectations. She directed some of her nervous energy into showering and fixing her hair and makeup with extra attention.

Her mom had been right about the weather; it had been a warm spring day. Christy carefully scrutinized her wardrobe. She had only five minutes before Todd was supposed to arrive, not that he was ever on time.

He tended to be pretty casual about everything. He usually wore shorts—even in the winter. He would probably have shorts on tonight.

Christy decided on her baggy shorts with her favorite red knit sweater.

Rick thinks I look good in red. Does Todd think the same thing? she wondered.

She pushed up the sleeves and took one last look at herself in her bedroom mirror before scooping up her ID bracelet from the dresser and fastening it securely.

"You smell good," Mom said as Christy cheerfully set the table for five. "What is that perfume?"

"Amazon Gardenia. Remember, I got it for Christmas? I'm almost out." Then she thought but didn't add, *I've been saving the last few squirts for when I see Todd. He told me once when I had it on I smelled exotic.*

"Do you think Todd likes lasagna?" Mom asked. "I've never

served it when he was here."

"I'm sure he does. You know how he always says the worst part about living with his dad is that he lives on microwave dinners. Besides, Todd likes whatever you make."

Christy thought it funny that even her mom wanted to please Todd. He had a way of making people feel like doing nice things for him.

As an only child whose divorced dad traveled all the time, Todd impressed adults as being more responsible and independent than most 17-year-olds. Without trying to, he also seemed to make adults want to lend him a helping hand, just because he was such a "nice young man," as Aunt Marti would say.

"Oh, someone called while you were in the shower. David took the message," Mom said, slipping on a pot-holder mitt and sliding a cookie sheet full of garlic bread into the oven.

"Who was it?"

"I don't know. Ask David. He's out front."

Christy stepped out onto the front porch and yelled for her brother, who was nowhere in sight. She caught a whiff of tiny white jasmine blossoms climbing up the trellis by the porch and remembered how awful this rental house looked when they'd moved in last September. The only thing on its barren porch then had been a smashed clay pot. Mom had done amazing things with hanging and potted plants, and Dad had built a trellis archway at the front steps.

The jasmine seemed to be twisting its way up the trellis a few inches more each day. She thought of how romantic it would be one starry night this summer for Todd to escort her up those steps and kiss her good night under the fragrant canopy.

"David!" she called. *What if it was Todd calling to say he would be late?* "David!"

"What?" He appeared from around the side of the house with one of the neighborhood kittens in his arms.

"Who called? Mom said you took a message."

"It was that guy."

"What guy?" Christy asked impatiently.

David dangled a long blade of grass above the kitten as it eagerly batted away at it. "I wish Dad would let me keep this one."

"David! Who called? Todd?"

"No, that other guy."

"Rick?"

"I guess."

"David! What did he say?"

"I'd call her 'Boots' if I could keep her, 'cause see?—she has white on her feet."

In one swift motion, Christy glared into her brother's face, grabbed him by the shoulders, and in a stern, controlled voice said, "What did Rick say, David?"

"I dunno. I told him you couldn't talk because you were grounded."

"I was grounded!" She dug her fingers into his shoulder. "Why did you tell him that?"

"Oww!" David jerked away from her grip and edged a few steps back, holding the kitten in tight defense. "What was I supposed to tell him? That you were in the shower? That's gross!"

Christy stared at her brother in disbelief. Sucking in a deep breath to compose herself, she stated, "Why don't you try telling the truth next time? Honesty is the best policy. Don't they teach kids these things in third grade anymore?"

David scrunched up his nose in his hamster look as his glasses slid down his nose. Her comments seemed to be beyond his understanding.

Feeling pleased with her self-control, Christy calmly said, "Okay? Do you understand? Next time, you tell the truth. Got it?"

Whether David "got it" or not didn't matter at the moment. The kitten decided to make a fast getaway and scratched David's arm in its exit.

"Come back, Boots!" David yelped, running after the tiny flash of fur.

Christy stayed out front on the porch a few more minutes, enjoying the evening breeze and watching for Todd's familiar VW bus. Plucking a jasmine blossom from the vine, she twirled it between her thumb and forefinger, drawing in its wild, sweet fragrance.

Should I call Rick back? she thought idly. *He probably wanted to make sure I went to practice after his pep talk. I don't want to be on the phone with Rick when Todd comes. Tonight belongs to Todd. Todd, where are you?*

Todd, unpredictable Todd, arrived more than half an hour late. The family had given up waiting for him and had sat down to dried-out garlic bread and mushy lasagna. Then they all recognized the familiar sound of Gus the Bus chugging to a halt in front of the house.

"I told you if we started to eat he would show up," David said proudly, jumping out of his chair and opening the screen door wide in an eager welcome. "Did you bring your skateboard?"

"Not this time, dude."

It happened again. It always happened. Whenever Christy heard Todd's easygoing, deep voice, something inside her stirred. The sensation was the same feeling she had on a hot summer day when she dove into a sparkling pool and felt that immediate, exhilarating splash of cool water. It took her breath away.

"Smells great in here! Italian?" Todd's six-foot frame entered the room, his sandy-blond hair windblown, his silver-blue eyes scanning the dinner table. He had on shorts, as Christy had predicted, and a white T-shirt with a volleyball logo on the pocket. In his arms he held a bright yellow produce box.

"What's in there?" David asked, straining to see into the flat box.

"Strawberries. You know that fruit stand off Highway 76? They were closing up for the day, but I talked them into selling me their last flat."

Christy could believe it. Todd could talk anybody into anything.

"Check 'em out," he said, holding up a strawberry as large as a small plum. "Vista is the only place I know where the strawberries grow like this. Sweet, too. Try one, dude."

David willingly shoved the entire strawberry into his mouth and gave a muffled "Mmmm-mmm!"

"How thoughtful of you, Todd," Mom said, rising and taking the flat from him. "Please sit down. I'm sorry we started without you."

"Hey, no problem. I'm just glad David saved some for me." Todd grinned at David, who returned a huge, beaming smile of admiration at his hero.

Todd sat down next to Christy, and she asked him, "Why did you go through Vista?"

"Tried to beat some of the traffic. I picked the wrong time of day to head south on the 5 freeway. How are you, sir?" Todd stretched out his hand to greet Christy's dad with a handshake.

"Fine. You'd better dig in there and get yourself some dinner."

Dig in he did. Christy had never seen anyone eat so much at one sitting. More than once, Todd said, "You're a great cook, Mrs.

Miller. This lasagna is incredible!"

Mom loved the compliments, of course, and it made Christy feel even more secure about how much her parents liked Todd. She knew for certain that things would work out, and she and Todd would go to his prom. There was no way her dad would say no.

Mom rinsed off several baskets of strawberries and served the fruit in bowls with puffs of whipped cream from the dairy where Dad worked. As Todd promised, the strawberries tasted sweet and fresh; they seemed to evaporate in minutes.

Whenever Todd joined in one of their family meals, it always made the conversation more lively, and they always sat around the table longer. It didn't matter what they were talking about. Sometimes Todd had stories about what had happened during the week. Sometimes David tried to be the center of attention, and everyone let him because Todd didn't seem to be bugged by David at all.

A few times Christy had held all of their gazes as she told about her week. Each time she did, her mom would say, "I didn't know that." Or, "You didn't tell me. When did that happen?" It always made Christy feel as though she'd hurt her mom's feelings for not confiding these bits of information the moment they occurred. It was as if she'd been holding out or trying to keep a secret from her parents. And she wasn't.

The truth was, most of the time the incidents weren't that important or that memorable. It was just that when Todd started talking around the table, it always made her think of other things to talk about.

Tonight Todd was giving a rundown of how Gus the Bus had sprung a leak in one of the hoses earlier in the week and how complicated it had been to find the right size replacement hose.

They chatted until David got bored with talk of car repair and excused himself from the table. Christy got up and began to clear the table. As much as she enjoyed sitting around talking like this, she was eager to be alone with Todd so they could talk about a few certain topics that were more interesting than leaky hoses.

Todd stood to help her clear the dishes, as he often did, and suddenly he said, "I was wondering, Mr. and Mrs. Miller, if you would mind if I took Christy someplace."

Christy stopped midstep into the kitchen and held her breath. *He's going to ask me to the prom like this? In front of everyone, with my hands full of dirty dishes? Todd!*

Mom flashed a look at her husband and then back at Todd. "What did you have in mind?"

"I wondered if we could go out for some ice cream or something. It's a great night for a walk. Is there any place close?"

Christy released her breath and lowered the dishes into the sink. *How romantic! He's going to take me out for a walk and ask me to the prom. Under the jasmine! I'll get him to ask me under the jasmine.* Her mind raced on ahead, her hopes soaring.

"I'm going, too!" David announced, jumping up from the couch in the living room.

"No you're not!" Christy snapped. "I mean, you probably should stay home; shouldn't he, Mom?"

Everyone looked at her. Christy realized she'd overreacted. There was no doubt from anyone in this room that she wanted to be alone with Todd. She felt as though they had all read her deepest, most secret wishes as easily as if they had been written on her face in fluorescent letters. Mom looked at Dad. He paused.

"Please?" David pleaded. "Can I go, too?"

"It's all right with me," Todd offered, standing between the kitchen and the table like a net over which passed a volley of looks between Christy and her mom, Christy and her dad, David and his dad. Todd held the empty lasagna pan in his hands, and in that moment Christy wanted to rub his face in the smeared tomato sauce.

How can you say it's okay for David to come with us? she thought angrily. *Todd, work with me here. I'm trying to get some time for just us.*

"I think," Dad said slowly, "that you need to stay around here, David."

"Aw—" David began in protest. Before he could say anything else, Dad gave him a look that silenced his complaining.

Now Christy was afraid her dad was going to say no to her as well, and she'd have to try to be more mature than David and hide her disappointment in front of her dad and especially in front of Todd.

But Christy's dad surprised her. "Christy, you and Todd can go over to Swensen's at the Vineyard, but I'd like you home before it's dark. Nine o'clock at the latest."

"Thanks, Dad." Christy tried not to sound too exuberant. She was sure her face showed her relief and delight, so she turned away from Todd so he wouldn't see her cheeks turn rosy.

Usually, when Todd came to see her, they did stuff around the house. Todd seemed more and more like one of the family. This was good, though. Very good. If Christy's dad didn't mind their going for a walk and for ice cream, then he probably wouldn't object to their going to the prom. Perhaps her dad realized something of which Christy was becoming more and more sure: She and Todd were ready to move forward in their relationship.

Todd stepped over to the sink and began to rinse off the dishes.

"I'll do those," Mom insisted. "You two get going. You only have an hour or so."

"Great dinner," Todd said, giving her a broad smile. "Thanks."

"You're welcome, Todd. You're always welcome. You know that. And thank you for the strawberries."

"Hey, dude," Todd called to David, who had flopped back on the couch, arms folded across his chest, glasses falling down, pouting like an expert, "you and I can do something together next time."

"When?" David stuck his lower lip out even further.

"Next time I come down."

"Can you come next weekend?" David looked up hopefully. "Can you come on Saturday? And can you come for the whole day?"

"Naw, can't come next Saturday."

"Why not?"

"It's my school prom that night."

David resumed his pouting, but Christy's heart stopped. *There, he said it! The prom is next Saturday. He's going to ask me to-night, I just know it!* But then Christy's thoughts swung sharply to the other side. *Next Saturday? That doesn't give me much time! Try-outs are Friday! When am I going to have time to get a dress and every-thing? Why didn't he ask me sooner?*

"Ready?" Todd broke into Christy's teeter-totter thoughts.

"Oh yeah. Sure."

For the first time that night, Todd's gaze fully met hers. He kept looking at her a bit longer than necessary, and Christy won-dered, *Am I doing it? Am I giving Todd a killer-eyes look, as Rick said? Does he feel for me what I feel for him?*

"We'll be back by 8:30 or 9:00," Todd called over his shoulder as he held the door open for Christy. "Later, dude!"

The screen door slammed behind them, and they heard David whine, "It's not fair!"

Todd and Christy smiled at each other and headed down the front steps and under the arch of climbing jasmine.

CHAPTER FIVE

An Enchanted Evening

Some spring evenings can be enchanted. Especially when the birds sing a little longer, and the colors of the sky pale into ethereal shades. When the wind snatches fresh blossoms from the trees, festively tossing them into the air like confetti, it's clear that it's a night for celebrating. Tonight was such an evening.

Not enchanted in a magical way, but in Christy's awareness that everything around her breathed with evidence of a living God. A God who thought up daffodils and the scent of grass and transparent rainbows in lawn sprinklers. A God who knew and cared about the hidden, treasured dreams of a young woman's heart.

Adding to the enchantment was the comfortable silence between Christy and Todd as they walked the first block. It usually was this way with Todd. He would often be quiet for a long while and then say something deep and wonderful. His conversations tended to be thought out and deliberate. Christy could talk on and on when she wanted to, but by nature she was more reserved and quiet, too.

One of the things she always liked about Todd was that he never made her feel uncomfortable because of her quietness during moments like this. Christy wondered now what he was thinking. Should she reach over and take his hand? She let her arm dangle close to his, hoping he would notice and mesh his fingers with hers.

"Did I tell you that I'm being discipled?" Todd said. "By a guy at church."

"What do you mean by 'discipled'?" Christy asked, moving a smidgen closer as they walked on.

"Well, we meet once a week and study the Bible together and help each other memorize verses," Todd explained. "You want to hear my verses?" He looked eager and excited, like a little boy who had something to recite for class.

"Sure," Christy said.

"It's First Corinthians 13. It's called 'The Love Chapter,'" Todd said.

Then, without Christy's expecting it, he reached over and took her hand. She closed her eyes for just a moment, determined to mark this moment in her memory very clearly so she could write about it in her diary that night. She couldn't imagine anything more romantic in the whole world than holding hands with Todd on an enchanted spring evening, listening to him recite what God had to say about love.

Todd began. "'If I speak with the tongues of men and of angels, but do not have love, I have become a noisy gong or a clanging cymbal. And if I have the gift of prophecy, and know all mysteries and all knowledge; and if I have all faith, so as to remove mountains, but do not have love, I am nothing. And if I give all my possessions to feed the poor, and if I deliver my body to be burned, but do not have love, it profits me nothing.'"

He paused, and Christy thought, *This doesn't sound very romantic.*

Todd went on. " 'Love is patient, love is kind, and is not jealous; love does not brag and is not arrogant, does not act unbecomingly; it does not seek its own, is not provoked, does not take into account a wrong suffered, does not rejoice in unrighteousness, but rejoices with the truth; bears all things, believes all things, hopes all things, endures all things.' "

He paused again and said, "That's all I know so far, but there are more verses."

Now it was Christy's turn to ponder her words before responding. The verses weren't anything like she thought they would be. The only part she really caught on to was at the end about "hopes all things" and "endures all things." Those were qualities she felt she had become well acquainted with lately in cheerleading.

"Did it take you long to memorize all that?" Christy finally asked.

"We've been working on it a few weeks now. I'm not a very fast memorizer."

"I'm not a very good memorizer either," Christy said.

"It helps me to write it out on cards and carry them around with me," Todd explained. "I worked on it while I was driving down here. That's probably why it's still pretty fresh on my mind."

"You did a really good job," Christy said. She liked praising him. She loved being beside him like this.

Todd squeezed her hand. "Hey, do you know where we're going?"

"We turn down the next street, and it's about three blocks after that."

"What a great night!" Todd said, filling his lungs with the evening air. "Smells almost . . . tropical, exotic."

"Could be my perfume." She lifted up her wrists to his nose so he could smell them.

"Yeah! What is that?"

Christy told him, and he said, "Reminds me of Hawaii. You ever been there?"

She felt like saying, "Oh, sure! When would I have ever gone to Hawaii?" but she settled for, "No, but I'd love to go someday."

"My dad and I lived there for a couple of years."

"You're kidding! I never knew that."

"Yeah, I went to King Kamehameha III Elementary School in Lahaina."

"Where?" Christy laughed at the mouthful of names.

"It's on Maui. I loved walking to school because of all the plumeria trees. They smell like your perfume. I'm going back there this summer."

Christy stopped walking. Their arms went taut in the sudden space between them. "You are? This summer?"

Todd smiled at her reaction. "Yeah, or next summer. I'm not totally sure yet."

They resumed their walk, and Christy fired a string of questions at him. "What are you going to do there? What about school in the fall? Where are you going to college? Don't you need to work this summer?" Her mind added, *And what about me?*

"Man," Todd said playfully, "you sound like my mother. Are you sure you don't want to ask if I put on clean socks this morning?"

"I'm sorry. I'm surprised, that's all," Christy said with a smile pressing the surprise out of her expression. "I just thought you'd be at the beach all summer, you know, like last year."

Todd shrugged and said, "Might be. I don't know yet."

Christy held his hand a little tighter and kept her feelings to herself the rest of the way to Swensen's. The deep-down truth surfaced over and over again: *He's not yours to hold on to.*

She deliberately ignored the thought. Enchanted evenings are to be enjoyed, not analyzed. Besides, there had been plenty of other times when she and Todd had been alone and Christy had spent the whole time brooding and missed the adventure of being with Todd. Tonight she was determined to not let her mood overwhelm her and take her deep inside herself, away from Todd.

To keep the conversation going, Christy said, "So, tell me about Hawaii. What did you like about it? Where did you live?"

Todd talked about the simple life he and his dad experienced living on Maui and how the two of them were together all the time. He almost made it sound like an ideal childhood, which surprised Christy, since she'd often felt sorry for Todd, because his parents divorced when he was very young and because he didn't have any brothers or sisters. Todd didn't seem to have any regrets.

Christy loved listening to him tell about his childhood and was a little disappointed when they arrived at the ice cream parlor. When he let go of her hand to open the door and then didn't take it again once they were inside, Christy was really disappointed that their walk had come to an end.

"Know what you want?" Todd asked, reviewing the list of flavors above the ice cream counter.

Her instant mental response was, *Yes! You! I want you to be my boyfriend and take me to your prom. And spend the summer with me on the beach. That's what I want!*

"Umm, I'd like a scoop of Swiss orange chip in a bowl, not a cone."

The girl behind the counter went to Christy's school, but Christy didn't know her name.

Todd smiled at her and gave his usual greeting, "Hey, how's it going?"

The girl responded with straightforward flirting. Christy couldn't believe it. As if Christy weren't even there, this girl started asking Todd his name and why she hadn't seen him before. She suggested that if he came back at closing time, she would give him free ice cream.

Todd stood like a rock, seemingly unaffected by this pushy girl.

Christy swelled with jealousy. *How dare she act like that? Can't she see Todd is with me? Who does she think she is?*

"Hey, thanks," Todd said when she handed him his change.

The girl grabbed Todd's hand and said, "Remember, next time come at closing, and you won't have to pay for it."

Christy couldn't stand the sight of that girl's hand touching the strong hand that had warmed Christy's only moments earlier. She wanted to leave—to get out of there and go back to their walk, hand-in-hand. She wanted to have Todd all to herself, even if for only an hour.

But Todd wanted to stay. He directed Christy over to an open booth against the back wall. They ate in silence for a few minutes, Christy scooping up tiny spoonfuls and slowly letting them dissolve in her mouth. Todd had a shake, and when she had calmed down enough to focus on him, it reminded her of their very first "date" at an ice cream parlor in Newport Beach.

"Do you remember the first time we had ice cream together?" Christy asked in a soft voice.

"When was that?" Todd said.

Christy felt her emotions scrambling to be strong and secure. How could it be such a strong memory for her and something he needed to be reminded of? "Remember? Last summer after Shawn's party."

Todd's face clouded, and she realized Todd was being overwhelmed with another more powerful memory. That was the night his friend Shawn died.

"Oh, yeah," Todd said slowly.

Now Christy was the one who had brought a somber mood to their time together, and she knew Todd might retreat deep into himself the way she sometimes did. She quickly changed the subject. "So, how's the end of your senior year going? Are you getting excited about graduation and everything?"

The "everything" meant the prom, but Christy didn't want to come right out and say it.

"I've got only a few more weeks left. My mom called the other night and said she would fly out for my graduation, so that's pretty cool."

"That's great," Christy answered brightly. "I imagine it will be nice for you to spend some time with your mom."

Todd nodded.

Out of the corner of her eye, Christy saw the door open, and the familiar bouncy blur of Katie entered. Katie spotted Christy and zipped over to their booth, immediately sliding in next to her, without even noticing Todd.

"I can't believe you're here! This is so perfect! You'll never guess what happened? He said yes, Christy! Can you believe it? Lance said he'd go with me! You should have heard my mom. You'd think I'd won a gold medal or something!"

Christy looked at Todd and then at Katie and said quickly, "That's great! Katie, this is Todd; Todd, this is Katie."

"Oh!" Katie noticed Todd for the first time, and her eyebrows rose. "Oh! Todd? That Todd! *The* Todd! Hi! I thought you were

David! I mean, not that you were David, but that Christy had come here with her brother because who else would she come with? I mean, besides you?"

Todd responded with his typical chin-up nod and said, "How's it going?"

"Katie goes to my school," Christy said, feeling a little embarrassed at her friend's loud enthusiasm. "We go to church together, too. I've told you about Katie."

Todd nodded.

"And she's told me a lot about you, Todd," Katie said, wide-eyed. "But what are you doing here tonight?"

"Katie!" Christy laughed nervously at her friend's lack of tact. "I told you Todd was coming tonight for dinner."

"No you didn't," Katie retorted quickly. She seemed to catch a look in Christy's expression that caused her to take her voice down a notch.

With a big smile at Todd, Katie said, "Nice to meet you, Todd. Really. I kind of feel as though I already sort of know you because of all the stuff Christy has, you know, told me about you guys. Not that she's told me any of the really private, personal stuff. But you know, all the good stuff about you, and I think you're really great, I mean, according to what Christy has told me."

Katie caught her breath, then turning to Christy she flashed her green eyes and said between her teeth, "I thought you were grounded!"

Christy's expression asked, *What?*

Katie moved closer to Christy. She casually put her hand to her cheek in order to hide her mouth and spoke in a strained whisper. "That's what Rick said. Everyone went to the movies, and he said—"

"Excuse me," Todd said, getting out of the booth. "I'm going to get some water. You two want anything?"

"No," Katie said, turning to face Todd with a bright smile.

"No, thanks," Christy responded calmly, but everything inside her felt like exploding.

They both smiled pasted-on smiles and waited until Todd walked out of earshot. Then as if a starting gun had fired, they took off talking, fast and furious.

"My dumb brother told Rick I was grounded when he called today. But it's not true."

"That's Todd?"

"Yes."

"Christy! He's . . ."

"I know. He is."

"But he can't be here now. You guys have to leave."

"Why?" Christy asked, checking over Katie's head to see if the flirty girl at the counter was going to try and capture Todd's attention again.

"Rick thinks you're going to ask him to the prom!"

"Rick? Why?"

"Because I told him you were!"

"Katie!"

"This morning you said you were."

"I did not!"

"Yes you did! At the lockers. You said you asked your mom since it was his senior year and everything . . ."

Christy squeezed her eyes shut and let her head fall forward.

"Katie!" It came out like a muffled scream. "I was talking about Todd. Todd's prom at his school. Not going to our school prom with Rick!"

"Uh-oh!" Katie moaned, leaning back in the booth. "I told Rick you were going to ask him and that's why I asked Lance, so the four of us could go together."

Christy lifted her head and stared at her friend in disbelief. Katie ignored Christy's glare and perked up as if a brilliant scheme had just hatched over her head. "Wait! It'll work! You can go to both proms! With both of them. You could even wear the same dress. Nobody would know!"

"Katie, they're on the same night," Christy said slowly. "And my parents would never go for that. You know that. If I had a choice of even going to a prom—any prom—I'd go with Todd."

"I don't blame you, Christy! I mean you told me he was cute, but cute isn't the word. He's, well . . . he's . . ."

"I know," Christy said with calm returning to her voice. "He's not like any other guy you've ever met, right?"

"Exactly." Suddenly, Katie's expression went starkly sober. "Oh noooooo!"

Christy followed Katie's line of sight, and her heart stopped. Through the glass door, she spotted a group from her school, ready to enter the ice cream shop. And leading the group was Rick Doyle.

CHAPTER SIX

Inside, Outside

The small ice cream parlor exploded with male laughter as the guys pushed the door open. Christy and Katie watched silently, frozen next to each other like two ice cream bars in the take-home case.

Rick faced the guys behind him, keeping them laughing with his nonstop jokes. Rick didn't even see Todd right in front of him, balancing a cup of water in his hand.

Christy clenched her teeth and watched the whole fiasco as if it were a well-rehearsed act. Rick's arm barely tagged Todd's cup, but on impact, Rick spun with trained reflexes and used his right arm to block whatever it was that had just touched him. Todd, perfectly balanced as if standing on his surfboard, took the toppling of his water cup without flinching, then curved his back and tucked in his chin just in time to avoid contact with Rick's reflex-driven arm.

Katie gasped, and Christy grabbed her arm.

"Oh, man!" Katie wheezed. "Did you see that?"

Christy couldn't talk. This couldn't be happening.

"Whoa! Sorry!" Rick said, but he didn't sound as if he was. He sounded more as though he was embarrassed.

The other guys walked past Rick and Todd, and one of them laughed and said, "Surf's up, dude!"

Todd good-naturedly gave him a chin-up, it's-cool gesture.

Rick snorted an embarrassed laugh, then brushed past Todd. He quickly scanned the room, probably concerned to see who had noticed. Immediately, he spotted Katie and Christy. A strange, almost angry look spread over his face, and Rick plowed right over to their table.

"Thought you were on restriction," he said as though he had a right to be mad at Christy for being there.

"No, I . . . it . . . my little brother lied. I'm not."

Rick nodded slowly, as if trying to decide if he believed her or not. "I called you tonight."

"That's what I found out." Christy's gaze went past Rick to Todd, where he stood at the counter getting another cup of water.

The girl behind the counter had dashed to the other side to bring Todd a towel. She eagerly helped Todd dry off his shirt. Christy couldn't hear what she was saying, but she could clearly see Todd's face, so calm, so willing to let this girl, this pushy girl, make a fuss over him. *How dare she! How could he?*

"Katie, would you mind letting me talk to Christy alone for a minute?" Rick said.

Katie looked to Christy for an answer, but Christy gave her a blank response. She still couldn't believe all this was happening.

"Sure," Katie said slowly, sliding out of the booth.

Christy felt like grabbing her and saying, "Don't leave me, Katie! Not now! Get back here!"

Rick's long legs bumped the table as he seated himself next to Christy. "So," he said, turning to her and giving her his usual half smile, "Katie tells me your parents agreed to release you from the rule that you have to be 16 before you can date."

"Well, um . . . ah . . . " Christy could hardly think. The most awkward thing in the world was just about to happen. Todd was coming back to the booth.

"Katie explained it to me," Rick said confidently, one arm across the top of the booth, the other arm resting on the table. He moved closer to Christy. "Since it's the prom and my senior year and all . . . and Lance said his dad would pay for a limo for the four of us."

Christy wanted to disappear. She wanted to absolutely vanish.

Todd now stood before them. His expression was a mixture of questioning and confidence, with a pinch of hurt puppy around the eyes. Christy knew that if she gave Todd only the slightest shake of her head, he would walk away and let her have a private conversation with this guy Todd didn't know who had just made himself at home in their booth.

But Christy didn't want Todd to leave her alone. And she certainly didn't want him to go back and strike up another conversation with little Miss Overly Helpful at the counter.

With her gaze held steady on Todd, she tried to find some kind of calming smile deep inside. She pulled it out, pasted it on her still-numb face, and quickly said, "Hi, Todd. This is Rick. Rick, this is Todd."

Rick abruptly turned and looked at Todd. "Yeah, we met," Rick said. "Bumped into each other earlier."

"Hey, how's it going?" Todd said. He casually slid into the seat across from Rick and Christy, apparently certain that he wasn't interrupting anything important.

Rick stared at Todd, as if expecting him to leave them alone. When Todd didn't move, Christy could see by Rick's expression that he slowly was realizing that Todd and Christy were together and that he was the outsider. Rick pushed himself out of the booth with the same strong, swift motion an athlete would use to do calisthenics.

"I'll see you at church Sunday," Christy said. It was all she could think of at that moment, since Rick's awkward invitation to the prom had been cut off. She hoped with all her might that he wouldn't say anything more here or now about it. Her non-committal sentence would say something to both guys. To Rick, it would say, "I want to talk to you some more." To Todd, it would say, "This is just a guy from church. No big deal."

The two guys exchanged a few "cool" phrases, and Rick walked away. He didn't look back at Christy or acknowledge her statement about church on Sunday. The way he was acting it would never appear to Todd that he had been sitting there, trying to invite Christy to the prom with him. She decided that was good because it wouldn't make things uneasy now with Todd.

Yet it also made her wonder if Rick would just as soon forget the invitation as well. Last Christmas Christy and Rick had hit an uncomfortable bump in their newly growing relationship. He kissed her in the church parking lot—twice—and Christy had pulled away. The rest of that night Rick had ignored her. It was several weeks before they started talking again, and when they did it was as if they were starting all over again, as if nothing had happened. Neither Rick nor Christy had mentioned the kiss, nor had they kissed again. It was one of those memories Christy buried deep inside, since she didn't know what to do with it.

Now the memory was back, sparked by the way Rick was once again ignoring her. He strode across the room and blended in with his group of buddies, pulling a chair up to their table.

Christy still felt as though her heart hadn't begun to beat again.

"I'll call you tomorrow, Christy," Katie said, instantly appearing at their table, giving Christy a look that said a whole lot more than the five words that came out of her lips. "It was really great to meet you, Todd!" Katie patted him on the shoulder and added, "I hope to see you again sometime."

Todd smiled and said something about Katie coming up to Newport Beach with Christy someday. Christy didn't hear the exact words.

She was trying to casually glance over her shoulder. To her surprise, she caught Rick staring at her. He wasn't ignoring her as she'd expected, and he didn't look away when she looked at him.

Neither did she.

Rick gave her a strange look. Was he furious or hurt or jealous? Maybe he was trying to express with his face how deeply he cared about Christy. She couldn't tell. She had never seen that look on him before. And the strangest part was that he wasn't ignoring her as he had in the past. It was all very unsettling.

And what is my face telling him right now? she thought. *Does he still think I have killer eyes?*

Katie gently punched Christy in the arm and said, "And don't forget our little angels in the nursery Sunday." She explained to Todd, "Christy talked me into volunteering to help with the toddlers' Sunday school class."

"Wait a minute," Christy said, trying hard to pull her full attention back to their booth before either Katie or Todd noticed she'd been staring at Rick. "If I remember correctly, you were the one who talked me into it."

"Whatever," Katie said.

"I'll be there, don't worry," Christy said. She tried to flash a confident smile at Katie, but Christy could tell that her friend was reading her like a billboard.

"I'm going," Katie said. "I'll call you tomorrow, Christy."

Christy nodded. It was nice to have a friend who could recognize the agony she was in at this moment. Katie exited, saying good-bye to the people from school who'd entered with Rick. They all knew her and waved as she left.

"I guess we probably should get going, too," Todd said.

Christy wished there was a way to get out without having to go past Rick. But there was only one door, and Rick and his friends were between them and that door.

Todd led the way, winding through the thin trail between the tables and heading for the door. Christy purposely tugged on the bottom of her sweater and smoothed the back of her shorts. Anything to appear preoccupied so she wouldn't have to make eye contact with Rick. She could almost feel him watching her leave with Todd.

What must Rick be thinking right now? she wondered.

Todd opened the door for Christy. An overly eager, high-pitched voice from behind the counter called out, "Good-bye, Todd. Don't forget!"

Todd turned slightly to give a chin-up to the girl behind the counter.

"Don't forget what?" Christy asked. The question gave her the opportunity to look back at Todd and then glance over his shoulder at Rick.

Rick was talking with the guys at his table, leaning over as if telling them a secret. He wasn't watching Christy at all. For some crazy reason, that made her mad. Never mind the fact that she'd been doing the same thing, and ignoring him. It just didn't seem right for a guy to ask her to the prom and then 10 minutes later ignore her.

"She was reminding me about the free ice cream," Todd said.

He seemed so casual about the whole encounter with that irritating girl.

They were only a half a block from the ice cream shop when Christy decided to speak her mind. "Don't guys hate it when girls throw themselves all over them like that?"

"I guess," Todd said with a shrug. He had his hands in his pockets and didn't appear ready to hold hands with Christy at all.

"Todd, she's such a flirt!"

"Some girls are."

"But, Todd," Christy argued, picking up steam, "she was so obnoxious in there. And did you see how much makeup she had on? What a cake-face."

Todd abruptly stopped walking. They were standing in front of a Mexican restaurant. Pulling his hands from his pockets, he lifted Christy's chin with his right hand and shot his piercing silver-blue gaze into her eyes. In a voice that shook her and melted her at the same time, he said, "Chris, I want to tell you something, and I don't want you ever to forget it."

His touch on her upturned chin felt gentle, yet firm and decisive. All her confused thoughts began to drain through invisible holes in the bottoms of her feet. All that mattered at this moment was Todd and what he was about to say to her.

"God made her face."

Christy blinked and tried to take in the meaning.

"God made her, Chris. God made her face. It hurts me when someone makes fun of something God made."

He let go, but Christy remained frozen in place, trying to put his words together with a returning rush of her emotions.

Then, as if adding a P.S. to his statement, he said, "Don't you see? People look on the outside, but God looks on the heart."

It shook her. All the way to her core, it shook her. *How does Todd do that to me? Is he mad at me for what I said?*

They started to walk again, side-by-side, without any words between them. Once they were out of the shopping center and on the quiet, tree-lined street, Christy bravely reached over and looped her arm in his.

"I'm sorry," she whispered.

Todd took her hand and squeezed it. She felt warm and secure, and all the eager anticipation of this being an enchanted evening returned. It wasn't over yet. They could still stand beneath the jasmine. He could still ask her to the prom.

"Don't ever get too proud to say that to somebody, Christy."

"That I'm sorry?"

"Yeah. Only people with soft hearts say they're sorry. And soft hearts are the only kind of hearts God can hold in His hand and mold."

"Todd . . . " Christy drew herself closer to him. She spoke in a delicate, sincere voice: "I honestly don't know what I'd be like if God hadn't brought you into my life. You are like nobody else I've ever known. You will never know how much you mean to me."

Then something she hadn't planned on happened. Her eyes swelled with tears that couldn't be held back, and without warning, a throaty gasp escaped.

Todd stopped walking and put his arm around her. Gladly burying her face into his chest, Christy sobbed a few more tears, then started to laugh. Pulling away, she looked up at a startled Todd.

"Your shirt's already wet, mister," she said, wiping her damp cheek. "There's no room for my tears."

They both laughed as Christy dried her eyes. Hand-in-hand,

they continued the walk home.

What a stupid little outburst! Christy thought. *Why am I so emotional tonight? What is it with all these feelings for Todd and all the confusing feelings I still have for Rick? Am I losing my sanity, or is it normal to be so easily overwhelmed when it comes to guys? Especially guys that I really care about. And how do I know how either of these guys really feels about me? I mean, do their thoughts and feelings about me change as quickly?*

Then a reassuring thought overtook her: *Todd is just as comfortable with my tears as he is with my laughter.*

She wanted to tell him that, to try again to somehow express her deepest feelings for him. But if she tried, she felt certain she would start to cry all over again.

"I like holding your hand," Christy heard herself say. She hadn't planned it, but it seemed the most natural comment at the moment. Everything inside her could go on feeling like a broken-up jigsaw puzzle as long as Todd kept his strong, warm hand wrapped around hers. She could work on putting the puzzle together later, when she was alone. Right now she wanted to be with Todd and not off in the Land of If Only, with all her perplexing thoughts.

"You know what?" Todd said. "I like holding your hand, too. I was just thinking what soft hands you have."

Christy gave Todd's hand a squeeze, and they walked on in silence, the pastel sky giving way to dusk.

CHAPTER SEVEN

Jasmine and Other Poisonous Flowers

About a block from Christy's house, Todd said, "I need to be at work by 6:30 tomorrow morning. I should leave as soon as we get back to your house. Hope it's okay if I don't come in."

"Sure. Thanks for the ice cream and sorry about the tears and everything."

"No need to apologize for your tears, Christy. You know that." He smiled an easygoing, Todd smile, and Christy smiled back.

Inside, Christy was beginning to feel a rising wave of nervousness now that they were almost to her front door. She knew if he was going to ask her to his prom, it would be in the next few minutes. That's when she noticed that Todd's hand felt suddenly moist and clammy. *Could he be nervous about asking me to the prom? It's not like him to be nervous, but I guess there's always a first time.*

Then Christy wondered if maybe it was really her hand that had turned sweaty when she started thinking about the prom again. She willed her emotions to remain calm—to hang in there just a few more minutes. The last thing she wanted to do was go into another one of her emotional outbursts in their last few minutes together.

They were in front of her house, slowly shuffling up the sidewalk together, when Christy stopped precisely under the arched trellis. She picked off a white blossom of the night-blooming jasmine and twirled it beneath her nose.

"Mmmmm. You must love jasmine, too," Christy said.

"What?" Todd snapped, looking shocked.

She had never seen him look so startled. Christy laughed at his reaction.

"The jasmine," she said, waving the tiny flower in front of him. "It has a tropical, sweet smell, like those trees you said you liked that grow in Hawaii. By the school you went to."

"Oh, right! The plumeria trees. Yeah, this smells good, too. I like the way it's climbing up this thing," he said, admiring the trellis. "It'll be cool when it's covered with . . . " He paused and said the word as though it were enchanted: ". . . jasmine."

"I know," Christy said dreamily. "Won't it be gorgeous?"

Todd let go of Christy's hand and sat down on the top step. He cleared his throat and said, "You know how I told David that next Saturday is prom night?

"Yes." *This is it! He's going to ask me. Here under the trellis, exactly as I dreamed! This is so perfect!*

"I wanted to talk to you about it, but funny thing is, I wasn't sure how to say it." Todd leaned back on his elbows and looked up at Christy.

She felt giddy but tried to look calm as she seated herself next to him on the step. "Just say it, Todd."

"Okay."

Christy waited. She smiled sweetly at Todd, encouraging him to open his heart to her and say the words she was waiting to hear.

"I'm taking a girl from school."

Christy immediately bit the inside of her mouth on both sides to keep from screaming. Her smile remained exactly the way it was before Todd had said the words that shattered her whole world.

"I knew you'd understand and everything, but, I don't know . . . I guess sometimes girls get their feelings hurt over nothing." Todd tilted his head and waited for her to respond.

She had drawn blood inside her mouth. She could taste it. Quickly swallowing, Christy exercised all the control she could find and asked the first thing that came to mind. "Is it anyone I know?"

"No. I just met her a few weeks ago."

A few weeks ago? And you picked her over me? I can't believe this!

"You'd like her a lot. She's been a Christian longer than I have, and she's unbelievably strong in her walk with the Lord."

Inside, Christy felt as if she'd been shattered into a million pieces, the way a fine china plate would shatter if someone smashed it with a sledgehammer. But she kept smiling.

"It's pretty incredible that she's so tight with God after all she's been through. She was in a car accident last summer. Spent three months in the hospital. She's in a wheelchair. Probably will be the rest of her life."

Pity and envy collided inside Christy. Envy was the stronger of the two. *So what? Am I supposed to feel sorry for her? Is that what you feel, Todd? Pity? Or does she mean more to you than I do? How could you possibly want to take someone in a wheelchair to a dance? Why, oh why do you want to take her instead of me?*

With her last pinch of stability, she ventured another question to hide her pain. "What's her name?"

Absolutely the most horrible, devastating moment of Christy's evening arrived when Todd's lips curled into a contented smile, his dimple showing on the right cheek. With a faraway look in his eyes, he answered, "Jasmine. Her name is Jasmine."

Christy jumped to her feet, ready to fight. But who was she fighting? She felt as if an invisible monster had punched her in the stomach, forcing all the air from her. No words came. Her frozen arms didn't know which way to return a swinging punch.

Todd stood, too. "I knew you'd understand. Hey, let me know how your cheerleader tryouts go on Friday. I'll be praying for you." He gave her a brotherly hug and a quick kiss on the cheek.

Don't pray for me! Don't do anything for me! Leave me alone, Todd. Get out of my life and don't ever come back! Christy felt as though her heart would explode.

Todd waved and then hopped into the front seat of his old Volkswagen van. As Christy stood alone under the jasmine-covered trellis, Todd took off down the street in noisy old Gus.

Numbly, Christy made her way through the front door and past her parents, managing to mutter to them a few sentences about being tired. At last she stepped into her room and pressed the door closed, sealing herself in her private tomb.

She fell on the bed, grabbed Winnie the Pooh, and silently sobbed into his furry yellow body. When she came up for air, she realized that this was the stuffed animal Todd had bought her last summer at Disneyland. With a ferocious throw, Christy catapulted poor Pooh across her room, where he landed on a mound of dirty clothes.

Sitting up, still trembling and sniffling, Christy grabbed her pillow and hugged it close, wiping her tears on the pink-flowered pillowcase.

"He doesn't care about me. He never has. It's all a big lie, and I believed it," she told her soggy pillow. "He doesn't give a rip about what's important to me or what really matters. He doesn't

care! No matter how much I want him to, it won't change anything. He doesn't love me at all!''

Bubbling to the top of her emotions' cauldron came an ugly
truth. Christy didn't know if she was talking about God or Todd.
Which one didn't care? Which one had stopped loving her?
Both? Either? The two had been so closely intertwined in her life
up to this point that it seemed difficult to think of one without
thinking of the other.

"Okay," she coached herself calmly, "figure this out. You can
do it. Come on. It's going to be okay. It's going to work out. It
always does."

A wild burst of anguish pushed its way out of her throat, and
she quickly pressed her mouth into the pillow and sobbed.

When the tremor passed, Christy decided not to think about
it anymore. She would go to bed, and she would choose to let all
her feelings die. It was the only way for them to stop controlling
her like this.

First there was one thing she needed to do. Still wobbly, she
rose and slowly stepped over to her dresser. Lifting a Folgers coffee can from the corner of the dresser, she popped off the plastic
lid and prepared to dump its contents into the trash can. Those
dozen dried-up carnations, the very bouquet Todd had handed
her last summer before kissing her for the first time, were as dead
as she wanted her feelings to be. They were brown and withered
and there was nothing lovely about them anymore. In fact, they
were ugly—sad and ugly—and they needed to be thrown away.

She couldn't do it.

Instead, she removed the "Forever" ID bracelet from her wrist
and buried it deep in the mound of stale carnation petals. With
a snap, the plastic lid fit over the tomb of her dreams, and cere-
moniously, Christy tucked it into the deepest corner of her closet.

She placed Pooh bear on top to stand guard and stated solemnly, "Never again will I give my heart away so easily."

The next morning she felt exactly the same. Nothing had mellowed during her fitful night of half-sleep, half-senseless dreams.

Part of her felt stronger, though. The determination part. During the night she had pictured herself in her cheerleader outfit with Todd, Rick, and Renee watching her spring into the air and land with perfect precision. The ultimate cheerleader, that's what she was.

She would show all of them: Todd, Rick, and Renee, her parents and Katie. She would prove that she was important and desirable.

For more than an hour, she lay in bed and let her searing thoughts burn into her emotions. She refused to feel sorry for this Jasmine girl. She refused to ever, ever get her hopes up with Todd again. He was a friend. Nothing more.

The longer she lingered in bed, the more time she had to form a plan. She needed to do something to make the hurting go away. It occurred to Christy that all wasn't lost with Rick. She hadn't said yes or no at the ice cream shop. She had, of course, been thinking no the whole time he was there, but Rick didn't know that.

Going to the prom with Rick was a good plan, she decided. It would certainly help the hurt she was feeling over Todd, and it probably wasn't too late to make it happen, if she went to work on it quickly.

That resolved, Christy allowed herself to make plans about cheerleading. Staring at the ceiling, Christy drew in a deep breath and determined she would make the cheerleading squad, period.

As far as her hopes in God and the way she had promised Him her whole heart last summer, well, she didn't want to think about that. It would be easier to figure out where God fit in her life after next weekend, when the tryouts and the prom were behind her. First things first.

Christy's mom knocked on her door and entered. "Do you realize what time it is?"

Christy glanced at her clock. "I was just going to get up."

"Do you want to go to the mall with us? I'm taking David to get a new pair of shoes. Dad ran over to the dairy for a few hours."

"No. I'll stay here. I've got a lot to do."

"Just don't waste the whole morning away, okay? And can you unload the dishwasher and put the towels in the dryer for me? They should be done in the washer in about 10 minutes."

"Sure."

"Oh, and Katie called about 8:00. I told her you were still asleep and that you'd call her back later. She said something about not being surprised that you were still asleep after last night. What do you suppose she meant by that?"

Christy sat up in bed and stretched. "Todd and I saw her last night when we went for ice cream." Christy considered giving more details of why it was an exhausting experience, like mentioning that Rick was there as well, but she wasn't sure. It would be too complicated to explain. And since she wanted everything to be set up perfectly before she asked her parents about going to the prom with Rick, she thought this wouldn't be a good time to launch a discussion that might end up needing a lot of explaining.

"Oh," Mom said. "Well, don't forget about the towels."

"I won't," Christy said as her mom exited, closing the door behind her.

As soon as her mom and David left, Christy called Katie. She told Katie, rather calmly, that Todd was taking another girl to his prom, and so Christy was ready to move on and arrange things so she could go with Rick. They talked on the phone for almost two and a half hours, making elaborate prom plans—everything from how to smooth things over with Rick and present the idea to her parents, to what she and Katie would wear and when they would do each others' nails.

With their plan of attack settled, Katie returned to a topic Christy had so cleverly skimmed over in the beginning of their conversation.

"Are you going to write Todd a 'Dear John' letter or what?"

"No. What would I say? 'You're a jerk because you'd rather take this Jasmine girl to your prom instead of me'? Or 'Sorry I'm not a very strong Christian, and Jasmine is. I suppose you spiritual giants need to stick together'?"

"You know what I can't figure out?" Katie said. "How are they going to dance?"

"You got me. Maybe he's going to sit on her lap, and she'll wheel him around the floor. Or being such a gentleman, maybe he'll push her chair around in circles until she gets so dizzy that she sprays punch out her nostrils."

"Christy!" Katie acted shocked, but she laughed loudly. "That is so rude! What if you were her? Wouldn't you love it if a guy like Todd would come into your life and take you to the prom?"

"Of course," Christy mumbled. "And I would have loved it if Todd had invited me. But he didn't. He invited her. And he seemed real happy about it. You should have seen his face, Katie, when he said her name . . ." Christy stopped midsentence when a thought came to her. "Oh, no. I can't believe it."

"What?"

"I just remembered something I said." Christy felt herself sink into an unwelcome depression.

"Well, what?"

"When we got back to my house, we were standing under the trellis, and I picked a flower and said, 'I bet you love jasmine, too.' I meant the flower, the one I was holding for him to smell. But you should have seen his face! I can't believe I said that!"

"You didn't know her name was Jasmine."

"He's in love with her, Katie. I know he is."

"Oh, stop it. You know who you remind me of?" Katie went on before Christy had a chance to answer. "You sound like Renee in English last week when she was moaning over how Rick turned down her invitation to the prom. Only she was moaning over *you* being the 'other woman'!"

"She was?" Christy felt a strange sense of exhilaration.

"Don't let it go to your head. You have a better relationship with Rick than any other girl I know. I don't think you should mess that up. My advice is, give Todd a rest, and tomorrow at church we'll work out all the prom plans with Rick and Lance. You'll see. Everything will be fine." Then Katie added exuberantly, "This week is going to be a week to remember."

Oh great! Christy thought. *Just what I need—a week to remember.*

Then, because Christy heard her mom's car pull up in the driveway, she said, "I've got to go, Katie. My mom and David just got home."

"I'll see you tomorrow," Katie said. "In the toddler Sunday school class. Don't forget."

"I won't. Why do you keep reminding me?"

"Because I know you, and when you get too much on your mind, you tend to forget some of the more obvious things in life."

"I do not," Christy protested.

Just then Mom walked in the front door with two shopping bags in her arms. She took one look at Christy lounging on the couch, still wearing her pajamas, and said, "Did you put the towels in the dryer?"

Christy closed her eyes and made a pained expression to demonstrate she'd forgotten. One of her mom's major pet peeves was towels that smelled mildewy because they'd sat too long in the washing machine out in the garage.

"How can you deny that?" Katie continued, apparently unaware of the moment of truth between Christy and her mom. "You know you forget things, Christy. Admit it."

"Okay, okay! You're right. I admit it. I've gotta go now Katie. Bye." She hung up the phone and sprang from the couch. "I'll do it right now, Mom."

"Don't bother," Mom said, putting down the shopping bags and hustling toward the garage. "I'm going to run them through a second rinse." She was shaking her head as she walked away. At the door that led into the garage, Mom stopped, and turning with her hand on her hip, she said, "I don't understand, Christina Juliet Miller, how you can manage to have such a selective memory."

Before Christy could defend herself, her mom said, "Would you please get yourself dressed now and empty the dishwasher?"

"Okay," Christy said quickly. She couldn't stand moments like this when she knew her parents were disappointed with her. As a child she rarely disobeyed her parents outwardly. But she knew she often disappointed them, like now. And this feeling in the pit of her empty stomach was worse than any punishment she could have ever received for disobedience.

The worst part of her realization was that this was not a good step in paving the way with her parents before convincing them that she should go to the prom.

Hurrying to her room, Christy dressed, made her bed, picked

up her dirty clothes, and then unloaded the dishwasher. She also made peanut butter sandwiches for herself, her mom, and David without being asked. Then she folded the towels after they'd finally tumbled dry.

Even though Christy knew her mom wasn't expecting her to do all these things to make up for forgetting earlier, she felt it was the least she could do. Her mom worked part-time at a real estate office and that made the weekends anything but restful for her because so many household chores had to wait until Saturday to be done.

One lesson her parents had tried to get across to her over and over was that if she wanted more privileges and freedom as she got older, it was up to her to show them that she was responsible. She knew that was part of their tactic in making her pay for half of her cheerleading expenses. And she had every reason to believe it would be a huge factor in their decision about letting her go to the prom with Rick. She had to do everything she could to prove to her parents that she was responsible.

Katie called again that afternoon, but Christy told her she couldn't talk because she was about to mop the kitchen floor.

"Mop the kitchen floor?" Katie asked.

"Yes," Christy said firmly, "mop the kitchen floor. I'll talk to you tomorrow."

When Christy met Katie in the toddler Sunday school class the next morning, Katie was ready to put their prom plan into action.

"Did it work?" Katie asked, her green eyes full of sparkles. "Did you mop your way to a yes from your parents?"

Christy opened her mouth to answer, but before any words came out, they were interrupted by a circumstance that happened to have the feeling of a miracle about it. However, since Christy wasn't exactly on speaking terms with God at the moment, she refused to acknowledge it as such.

Mrs. Johnson, one of the mothers, stepped up to Christy with her three-year-old daughter, Ashley, in her arms.

"My daughter has talked about you all week long," Mrs. Johnson said.

Ashley played shy on her mommy's shoulder. Christy gave her a grin and reached out for her. Ashley gladly hopped into Christy's open arms.

"Look," the little cutie said, holding up a Band-Aid-wrapped finger. "I got an owie."

"She stuck her finger in her brother's pencil sharpener," Mrs. Johnson said.

"Aw." Christy kissed it and asked, "All better?"

Ashley nodded, her blond ponytail bobbing up and down.

"I was wondering, Christy, if you'd be available to baby-sit for me sometime?" Mrs. Johnson asked.

"Sure."

"Oh, good. We can talk about it some more later, but I'm going to need a full-time baby-sitter during the summer. If that might work out for you, let me know. Ashley adores you."

Mrs. Johnson left, and Ashley scooted down to make herself at home with two little boys in the play kitchen.

Had to be a coincidence, Christy thought. *Or maybe my mom knows her and told her I needed a job to pay for cheerleading.*

The next hour and a half zoomed by with little-kid activities scurrying all around Christy. The room full of toddlers demanded her complete attention, and she and Katie barely talked to each other.

One little boy sat by himself most of the morning. He wore glasses strapped over ears that were too big for the rest of his head. The combination of his ears, glasses, and strap made him look peculiar.

He finally joined the other tots toward the end of class, when paper and crayons were passed out.

"You made a funny picture," another boy said when the little guy in glasses held up his work.

"I did not!"

"Yes you did! It's funny."

The boy burst into tears and, poor thing, couldn't get to his eyes because of the strapped-on glasses.

Christy and Katie both went immediately to the scene, since the teacher had her hands full with a wildly kicking toddler in the corner.

"What's the problem here?" Katie asked firmly.

"He made fun of what I made," the wounded boy cried.

Sober-faced and appearing innocent, the other child explained, "I only said it was funny because it is."

"But you made fun of what he worked hard to make," Katie said, lifting the crying boy while Christy went for a tissue. "Tell him you're sorry."

"No."

"You need to tell him you're sorry."

The boy froze, defiant and determined not to say the words.

Katie forced the issue by using a stern voice and an angry look. "You say you're sorry. Now!"

"Sorry." A peep from a chick would have come out louder.

Katie seemed satisfied that justice was served, and she left the coloring table because the first parents were arriving to pick up their children.

Christy, about to walk away, heard the defiant apologizer say in a low voice, "You have funny ears and a funny face!"

The memory of Friday night with Todd rushed upon her. Christy spun around and looked sternly at the tot.

In a quiet, firm voice, she said, "Don't you ever make fun of what God made. Do you understand me? God made that little boy. Don't you dare make fun of him!"

The boy sat perfectly still, his head down. Christy realized her words had frozen the little guy. She had used the same words Todd had, but the way Todd had said it had melted, not paralyzed, her.

Christy wanted to walk away from it all. It felt awful quoting Todd, especially when she wanted to still be angry at him. She didn't want Todd to be right about anything, and she detested the way she had imitated his spirituality.

She busied herself by sorting toys, cleaning them, and placing them in the appropriate boxes. This gave her time to calm down and sort through her feelings, putting them back into their appropriate boxes.

She didn't see the little guy with the big ears sneak up behind her. He tugged on her skirt. Christy turned and looked into what could have been the face of an angel; his expression shone. His smile, so wide and so sincere, overshadowed the glasses and large ears. He looked up at her as if her reprimand to the bully had changed his life.

"Bye, Teacher," he said in a squeaky voice. Then he galloped over to the door, where his father stood waiting.

People look on the outside. God looks on the heart. As much as she hated her thoughts and the way they forced more of Todd's words to the front of her mind, she let them linger a brief moment, remembering the little boy's smiling face.

CHAPTER EIGHT

Prom Plans

Katie got Christy's attention and motioned from the door to the classroom. "Come on. Let's go."

The two girls slipped out of the toddler room and into the bathroom to check their hair before beginning step one of their prom plan.

"Okay," Katie began, "it's by the book now, Christy. Just as we planned yesterday. Lance is going to be waiting for us, and you let me take it from there."

"But Katie—" Christy began.

"I don't want to hear it," Katie interrupted. "This is no time to turn fainthearted on me. Come on. Exactly as we planned. Follow my lead."

They stepped out of the bathroom, and there was Lance, waiting for them as Katie had predicted. Lance was a unique guy. He dressed wildly—always. And his hair changed week to week, not only the style but usually the color as well. One thing could be said for Lance: Everyone at school knew him, and most people knew he was supposed to be a Christian. At least he was really involved in the youth group.

"There you are," he said dramatically, offering Katie his arm.

"May I escort you to church?"

Katie played along with the dramatics, which Christy thought looked kind of cute for those two.

"Have you seen Rick?" Katie asked, giving Christy a glance over her shoulder. "We need to check and make sure everything is all clear with him, you know, about making it a foursome on Saturday."

"He's around here someplace. Let's go find him." Lance spoke like some kind of cartoon character. Then he did a little hop and walked off like Charlie Chaplin.

The church hallways filled with people moving to and from classrooms and the sanctuary. The three friends stayed together and found Rick talking to a group of girls out front.

When Rick saw them, he kept talking, indicating that the group he now entertained carried more importance than the threesome approaching him. Christy started to feel more nervous than she thought she would. This whole thing wasn't settling well inside of her.

Katie took over as only Katie could. "Yo, Doyle! Get your brown eyes over here. We have plans to discuss."

Suddenly, Christy lost all nerve. Going after guys like this had never been her style. She wished she had never agreed to Katie's prom plan.

Too late now. Rick sauntered over, cool, calm, and confident. Christy thought how great Rick would be for a deodorant commercial. He had a "nothing-can-faze-me" look on his face. Christy, on the other hand, felt like a perspiring mess. Rick gave Katie and Lance a smile but deliberately did not make eye contact with Christy as they talked.

Is he mad about Friday night and Todd? Or is it my killer eyes? Is he afraid to look at me because he might read something deep and desperate in my eyes? Is that what I am? Desperate? I must be. At least I'm desperate enough to let my friend run my dating life for me, such as it is. Oh, this is really getting pathetic. I wish . . .

Before Christy could complete her "wish," Katie had sewn up the prom plans, and in less than three minutes. All that needed to be decided was what time the limo would come by to pick them up. It had to be a world's record in persuasive speech. Katie even told Rick to get flowers that would go with a red dress, since she had heard he liked Christy in red.

Why did Katie blurt that out? How embarrassing! Christy thought. *And where am I going to come up with a red dress by Saturday?*

Rick's glance finally fell on Christy, and he jokingly said, "Not going to cause waves with Moondoggie, am I?"

"Who?" Christy scanned her memory until she remembered that Moondoggie was the name of a surfer in an old beach movie. She forced a laugh with the others and shook her head. "No."

"Believe me," Katie said. "There's no chance of that relationship surviving. 'Moondoggie' is long gone."

Rick's gaze shot directly to Christy's wrist, where the ID bracelet she had worn since New Year's was now conspicuously absent. She never knew Rick had noticed it before. Only her girlfriends knew Todd had given it to her.

"Is that right?" Rick said. His charming smile showered Christy with his approval. He wrapped his arm around her and pulled her to his side. "Good," he said in a low voice. "Really good."

So it was decided. They were a foursome for the prom, and to make it official, they all walked into church together and sat where everyone could see them.

Christy didn't hear a word of the service. At this moment she knew of nothing she wanted to hear from or say to God.

By the time church let out, Christy had convinced herself that all of this scheming and forcing together of the pieces was fine. So what if she didn't have Todd and those dreams; she could make this prom plan work! She would go with Rick and be beautiful and have a wonderful time, and everyone would be happy for her. Everyone except one person whom she forgot to include in the prom plan.

Her dad.

"No, Christy. Absolutely not," he said at the kitchen table after their Sunday meal. "You are not going to any prom. It's completely out of the question."

Christy went on as if she hadn't heard him. "But, Dad, it's not really a date because four of us are going together, and see, they're counting on me. Lance's dad already rented a limo for us."

"A limousine?" Mom blurted out. "I don't understand you, Christina! Did you think for one minute that your father and I would ever approve of your going to a prom? And in a limousine?"

"Well, I thought maybe you'd make an exception because I'm going with my friends from church, and like I said, it's not really a date."

Mom and Dad looked at each other as if silently urging the other to go first. Christy still felt she could persuade them, so with polite persistence she asked, "Could you just explain to me why I can't go?"

"For starters, you're not allowed to date until you're 16," Mom said.

"And," Dad cut in, looking upset, "we don't approve of proms and dances."

"But why?" Christy asked.

"The music—"

Mom cut in. "We don't let you listen to that kind of music at home. Why would we let you go to a dance and listen to it all night?"

Dad pressed on with his list. "And the atmosphere, the way the girls dress, and the . . ." He cleared his throat. "The suggestive dancing. The answer is no, Christy. You're not going."

"What if I went, but I promised not to dance?" Christy turned to her mom, hoping for support. But Mom's gentle face had a firm, set expression.

"That's not the whole issue, Christy. Other parents from church may let their kids go," she said, "but your father and I don't want you to go. You will have to tell this boy that you can't go."

"I can't." Christy's voice came out in more of a whine than she had intended.

"Of course you can. You simply tell him, 'Thanks for asking me, but I can't go,' " Mom coached.

"But he didn't exactly ask me. I, well, I kind of asked him."

Mom stared at Christy. "You did what?"

"I kind of asked him. Actually, Katie asked him for me, because she wanted to ask Lance. And she did, and so now we all have to go together."

Her father rose from the table, pressing his knuckles against the tabletop. "You handle this, Margaret. If I do, I'll regret it later."

He pushed away from the table, leaving Christy with a mother who looked flame-broiled.

"What's this boy's name?"

"Rick. Rick Doyle. You know him. Don't you? He's really nice, Mom."

"Do you have his phone number?"

"Yes."

Mom pressed her lips together. "I want you to call Rick right now and tell him you're sorry, but it was a big mistake and you're not going to the prom."

"I can't, Mom."

"Yes you can." The words came out evenly spaced and with quiet intensity.

Christy swallowed a lump of tears and pride. How could she possibly tell Rick she was sorry, but the plans were off?

It would be best to get it over with. The scariest moment of her life had to be the moment Rick answered the phone.

With her mother standing next to her, Christy forced out, "Rick? Hi, it's Christy."

"Hi, Killer. What's up?"

"Rick . . ." She couldn't do it. She couldn't tell him the plans were off.

"Yeah?"

Mom moved closer and said firmly, "Would you like me to talk to him?"

Christy shook her head and turned away slightly. Mom stepped back and waited.

"Um, Rick, something has come up, and well . . . I can't go to the prom."

Silence.

"I . . . I'm sorry."

Click. Dial tone.

Christy turned to her mom, holding out the buzzing receiver like a dead mouse. "He hung up!" She burst into tears.

Mom replaced the buzzing receiver and did her best to comfort Christy.

As she had been doing a lot lately, Christy swallowed back the onslaught of tears and tried her best to cover up her feelings. As much as her mom was trying to console her, it wasn't helping. Christy was anxious to be alone in her room.

Her mom let her go, saying, "I know it's hard, honey. I know it's hard."

Then why did you make me do it? What's so awful about going to one stupid little dance in my life? Why do you treat me like such a baby? You don't care about what's really important to me! You just don't care.

Christy flopped onto her bed, ready for a long cry. But her dad tapped on the closed door and let himself in. Christy wasn't sure if she should hide her feelings and turn off the tears, or go ahead and make a real scene. There was a wild, random flit of hope that if she threw a tantrum, he might change his mind. Not that he ever did change his mind, once he made his decision known.

She gave him a strange combination of the two options, turning an expressionless face to him. A face that said, *You can't hurt me. I won't let you.* The only problem was, the tears refused to turn off and cascaded down her cheeks.

Dad lowered himself to the edge of her bed, and the whole side sloped downward. Rubbing his hands on his lap, he began to string his words together.

Christy lay motionless, inwardly pleading, *Don't yell at me. Please don't tell me what a stupid mistake I made getting all wrapped up in this prom thing. Don't lecture me. Just hold me. Couldn't you just hold me and let me cry my heart out?*

He ran his big fingers through his thick, reddish-brown hair. "You know, things are different now from when your mother and I were your age."

She knew that.

"And some things are different here in California from Wisconsin."

She knew that, too.

"You need to understand that guys are different from girls."

She definitely knew that!

"I know what guys think about when they dance, especially nowadays with the suggestive words in songs—"

"Dad—" Christy tried to interrupt, but he had more to say. He held up his hand to silence her.

"I know how it is, Christy, and I don't want some guy thinking about my daughter that way. And I especially don't want my daughter trying to make herself fit into that kind of a . . . a . . . into that kind of environment."

Christy sniffed. The tears kept flowing.

"Your mother and I want you to be what you are and not try to be something you aren't. You're 15, not 16. And you're the daughter of a dairyman, not some movie star who rides around in limousines."

The way he said it sounded so absurd that a spontaneous cough-laugh popped out of Christy's throat. Her dad's face softened. His eyebrows relaxed, so they weren't as scrunched together.

"You're going to have to trust your mother and me, Christy. You may not like the decisions we make, but we're doing the best we know how."

"I know," Christy said softly, her heart turning a little bit tender. "I'm sorry. I got kind of wrapped up in my dreams. You know. It's important to a girl like me to be able to dream of getting all dressed up and feeling, well, really special. I need to feel that I'm special, Dad."

The statement surprised her. She hadn't realized it until she said it. It was the most deep-core, honest thing she had said to him in months. Maybe years.

"Nothing wrong with dreams," he said, still trying to look stern but not succeeding. "We all need to have dreams. The question is, does the dream control you, or do you control the dream?"

Christy nodded her understanding, blinking the final tears off her eyelashes. This felt good—talking to her dad almost as though they were both adults. And he hadn't even yelled at her. At least not yet.

Christy felt ready for a final tender moment with her father. Maybe she should try to explain to him the crazy thought she had just now. The thought that if he would make her feel more special, then maybe it wouldn't be quite so important to her that she got that kind of attention from other guys.

She didn't know how to tell him. But she knew what she wanted. She wanted him to hold her moist face in those huge, rough hands of his and kiss her on the forehead the way he did when she was little and he tucked her in at night.

But just then David knocked on the bedroom door.

"Christy, phone," he called.

"Who is it?"

"Some girl."

Christy made a face at her dad that said, "Little brothers!" He smiled.

"What's her name?"

"I dunno. I told her you were crying your eyes out in your room 'cause you were getting yelled at for not having a boyfriend."

"David!" Christy yelped and sprang from the bed, then shot a glance at her father. "Is it okay if I go see who it is?"

He nodded, and she was out the door, grabbing David by the shoulders. "Why did you say that?"

David trembled—a mocking kind of "Help, I'm scared!" tremble. His words matched his comic actions. "You told me to always tell the truth on the phone."

Christy brushed past the little clown and retrieved the dangling receiver. "Hello?"

"Christy?"

"Yes, this is Christy."

"Hello! How are you? This is Alissa!"

"Alissa? You're kidding!" Christy met Alissa on the beach last summer. They had written a few times but never called because Alissa lived in Boston.

"How are you doing, Christy?"

"Fine! How are you doing?"

"We're doing wonderful."

"We?" Christy ventured. "You mean you had the . . . I mean, you had your baby?"

"Last week. It's a girl."

"Really? That's great, Alissa."

"I named her Shawna Christy after you and, well, after Shawn. She's beautiful, but she doesn't have any hair yet."

Christy giggled along with Alissa. "You're doing all right, then?"

"Besides being 20 pounds overweight, yes. I'm probably doing better than ever before in my life, thanks to you."

"What did I do?"

"Christy, if you hadn't written me and encouraged me and told me that God cared about me and everything, well, when I found out I was pregnant, I probably would have killed myself or had an abortion, or I don't know what. I never would have gone to the Crisis Pregnancy Center. The only reason I went was because you kept telling me to go to church and meet some Christians. I knew I couldn't just walk into some church, pregnant and everything, and expect people to accept me."

Todd's words flashed before Christy and to get rid of them, she used them in her reply. "You know, Alissa, people look on the outside, but God looks on the heart."

"I know that now. That's what my counselor, Frances, tells me. She has a support group for expectant and new mothers at her home. I've been going every week. They talk about God a lot, and I'm starting to understand some of the things you told me in your letters about trusting God enough to give Him your heart."

The words stung. Right now Christy felt as though she and God were having a tug-of-war with her heart, and she knew she was winning. Apparently, Alissa and God were having the same struggle, only God appeared to be winning with Alissa. "Well, have you?"

"Have I what?" Alissa asked.

"Have you done that yet? Given God your heart?"

"Not exactly. Frances has explained it all to me: how I need to be sorry for what I've done to hurt God and ask Him for forgiveness and then surrender my life to Him. I just haven't done all that yet. It's always been hard for me to say I'm sorry, and I have an even harder time trusting someone to take control over my life, or however Frances explained it."

Christy felt disappointed. Ever since last summer she had wished Alissa would surrender her life to the Lord and become a Christian. She seemed so close to making the decision.

"How's Todd? Are you two still together?" Alissa asked, changing the subject.

"Not exactly."

"What's going on? Your brother said you were in trouble for not having a date or something."

"He got it all mixed up." Christy hesitated, then decided to tell all to this faraway friend who had been so transparent with her. She concluded the whole saga by adding, "And things with Todd are not very great. He's taking some girl named Jasmine to his prom next Saturday, and since she's in a wheelchair, he seems to think I should feel sorry for her, like he does."

"She's in a wheelchair?"

"Yes, from a car accident. She's probably got long, blond hair like yours, and I wouldn't be surprised if she's elected prom queen."

"Really?"

"Well, I don't know, but he's crazy about her, so I figure there must be more going on than he's telling me. I've put him on my list of 'just friends.' Besides, he might not even be around this summer."

"Where's he going?"

"Hawaii. Don't you feel sorry for him?" It came out as sarcastically as she meant it.

"I loved Hawaii when we lived there. My dad and I used to walk on the beach every night."

Christy knew Alissa's dad had died a year ago. She wondered if she should venture a question about Alissa's alcoholic mom.

"Are you still living with your grandmother?"

"No, she kicked me out a couple of months ago because I embarrassed her in front of all her proper Bostonian friends. She hasn't seen Shawna yet. Neither has my mom."

"How is your mom?"

"The same. She's been in and out of the same treatment program twice."

"So, where are you living?"

"With Frances's daughter. She's married to a really nice guy, and they have two little girls, so Shawna has built-in playmates."

"That's great! I'm so glad things are better for you."

"I think about you a lot, Christy, and how you said that God knows and cares about everything in my life. It's hard for me to believe, but I think about it a lot.

"Would you tell Todd hi for me? That is, when you start speaking to him again. Did I tell you he wrote me the most incredible letter a couple of months ago? Five pages long. I think I've read it 100 times. I'm going to save it forever and let Shawna read it when she's old enough."

Todd wrote her a five-page letter? He's never written to me!

"I really need to go," Alissa said. "And don't worry, Christy. Things with you and Todd will work out. They always do. But when you do talk to him, tell him I think he should have taken you to the prom."

"Right," Christy said. "I'll tell him." She said good-bye to Alissa, hung up, and added silently, "That is, if I ever speak with him again in my life."

CHAPTER NINE

Jealous Love

On her way up the front steps of the school building on Monday morning, a girl Christy barely knew came up to her and said, "Are you the girl who dumped Rick Doyle?"

"Excuse me?"

"I heard you gave Rick a taste of what he's always dishing out. Good for you!"

Christy ignored the girl's comments and entered the building. Out of the corner of her eye, Christy thought she saw Rick coming in her direction. She got up the nerve to look at him, but when she looked, he wasn't there. She didn't know if he'd turned and gone the other way in the crowded hallways or if it really hadn't been Rick to begin with, but she just expected to see him.

Someone bumped hard into Christy's shoulder as they passed in the hallway. She turned to recognize the girl as one of Renee's friends.

"What is going on?" Christy muttered. She hurried to meet Katie at their lockers as usual.

Katie gave her a cool look and said, "I don't know if I'm speaking to you or not."

"You too? Take a number. Or better yet, why don't you call

me and when I answer, you can hang up on me."

"What is that supposed to mean?" Katie said, giving Christy a disgusted look.

"I mean, I'm sorry. I know I messed everything up. I tried to tell you Sunday before the toddlers' class that I hadn't asked my parents yet, but then everything got going so fast . . ."

"You're trying to say this is my fault?"

Christy leaned against her locker and looked her friend in the face. "No, I'm not trying to say that at all. This whole mess is my doing. And I'm sorry it didn't work out the way we planned. I was hoping it would work out, Katie. I was dreaming big things. But my parents absolutely won't let me go."

"Are you sure?"

"Yes, I'm positively sure."

Katie seemed to soften. "You could have called me, Christy. It's pretty awful hearing it from one of Rick's friends."

"I'm sorry, Katie."

"What's worse is when I tell Rick's friend he doesn't have the story straight because I know what's going on and he doesn't, and then Rick walks up and says I'm wrong."

"Katie . . ."

"I don't know if I want you to apologize, Christy. You see, Rick's never been stood up before. I'd probably be more mad at you, except I think it was time he got some of his own medicine, and you were just the one to give it to him."

"I wasn't trying to—"

"Lance and I will have a miserable time without you, you know."

"No you won't! You two will have a wonderful time. Besides, isn't Rick going to go anyway?"

"How would I know? He's playing it so cool. Nobody knows

what he's going to do. Besides, why would he still want to go with me and Lance? He's not exactly friends with either of us."

The bell rang, and Katie gave Christy a playful slug in the arm. "Don't look so depressed. You've got to come up with a few smiles for cheerleading tryouts this Friday, you know. Wouldn't hurt to start practicing now."

Christy forced a pathetic grin.

"Never mind," Katie said. "Go ahead and be depressed all day today and get it over with. I'll check on your smile again to-morrow morning."

Christy shuffled to class. The luxury of being depressed all day didn't sound so bad.

"How was your weekend?" Liane, a girl in her algebra class, asked.

"It was interesting," Christy answered cautiously. She wondered who else knew about Rick. Liane didn't usually talk to her. Had her life become an open book at Kelley High School?

"Oh really? What was so interesting about it?" the girl probed.

"It was a hard weekend, that's all."

"Well then, I sure hope your week turns out better than your weekend!" Christy couldn't tell if the girl was being serious or sarcastic.

Class started, and Christy thought, *This week has to get better. Everyone is watching me! I have to work hard at tryouts, and on Friday I have to make the squad. It won't make up for the prom and Todd and Rick, but it'll show everyone that I did it. And I did it on my own.*

The algebra teacher passed out the corrected quizzes from Friday. He handed Christy hers first. A huge, red F had been circled on the top of the page. She had never received an F before. D's and Incomplete's but never an F. In horror, Christy discovered she had missed every problem. This was not the way to begin a week that was supposed to turn out better than her weekend.

"One-third of the class failed this exam. Those of you who did will need to take a makeup test," the teacher announced. "I'm giving the makeup tomorrow after school."

Oh great! How am I going to be in two places at once? Christy thought in frustration. *I need to be at practice, but if I don't make up this quiz, I'm in deep trouble. And when am I going to find time to study?*

Her troubles didn't get any easier at practice. Renee huddled with her friends, gossiping, and all three turned to look Christy over as she came on the field.

When Christy got close enough to hear, Renee said, "Well, at least my mommy and daddy are letting me go to the prom, not like some people we know who are still too young to play with the big boys."

The girls giggled. Christy ignored them, doing her stretching exercises by herself.

"Watch, she's going to admit she's too young to be a cheer-leader, too. Just wait. Yoo-hoo," Renee mocked, "change your diaper before practice? We wouldn't want any accidents, you know."

Christy closed it all out, pounding a single sentence through her mind over and over: *Ignore her. Ignore her.* Then she added, *I can do this. I can do this.* As the rest of the girls gathered, it became obvious the hopefuls had dwindled down to the determined. Eight girls remained. On Friday the judges would select seven cheerleaders. That meant all but one of them would be chosen.

The girls were highly motivated now, each trying to prove that she deserved to be one of the chosen seven. As they ran through the cheer a few more times, Christy concentrated on making her

arms the straightest, her moves the sharpest, her voice the loudest.

> We're on our way
> Straight to the top
> We'll never give up
> We just won't stop!

"Okay," Mrs. James reminded them after practice, "those of
you who are here today know that it's between you eight. We
might have one or two more who just couldn't come today. The
next three practices are crucial. Please be here for all three; oth-
erwise, I'm sure it will affect how you do on Friday. Any questions?"

Christy waited until the other girls had left before asking
about Tuesday. "I need to take a makeup test in algebra tomorrow," she explained, "and that's the only time he's giving it."

"It's up to you," Mrs. James said. "These last three practices
are the most critical. You're doing well, Christy, but I think you
need the practice. You'll have to decide which is the most important to you."

"I could help you," Teri said. She had stood up to Renee last
week and now she was being nice to Christy again. It was won-
derfully refreshing, after the way the rest of her day had gone. "If
you take the test and then come late to practice, I could stay after
and show you what you missed during the first part."

"Are you sure?"

Teri nodded, her brown eyes showing her sincerity.

"Is that okay, Mrs. James?" Christy asked, still amazed at
Teri's generous offer.

"It's up to you girls. I'll be here until 4:30. After that, you're
on your own."

"Thanks, Teri," Christy said.

"Sure. See you tomorrow."

That night Christy spent at least two and a half hours on her algebra. She decided not to tell her parents about the F. Why get them all upset when the teacher would be recording the makeup grade?

She busied herself with her homework until 10:00, trying hard to concentrate. Wanting to get her homework done was only part of the reason for plunging in so diligently. The other reason attacked her as soon as she climbed into bed.

It was her thoughts. And her feelings, which she had so carefully guarded in her heart. Churning around like sneakers in a dryer, her thoughts and feelings now bumped into each other in the darkness: Todd, Jasmine, Rick, Katie, Renee, and all the pressure she had put on herself to make the squad. All the issues in her life spun around in her subconscious through the night.

She didn't pray. She hadn't since Friday. She knew she would feel better if she did, but her stubbornness kept her from yielding. Instead she chose to stay motivated by anxiety and jealousy.

Katie noticed at lunch on Tuesday that Christy wasn't wearing her "Forever" ID bracelet. Christy told Katie that she would keep it as a memory, but it didn't really mean anything anymore.

"What are you saying?" Katie questioned. "That you've dismissed Todd from your life? I find that hard to believe. I thought you said once that he would be in your heart forever."

"Did I?"

"Yes, of course you did. You want to know what I think?"

"No." Christy bit into her peanut butter and honey sandwich, knowing that Katie would disregard her reply.

"I think you really, truly love Todd deep down, but you're afraid to get hurt because your relationship is so up and down."

"No, Todd's only a fantasy. I've wanted him to care as much about me as I care about him, but he's always been off in his own dimension. We're not good for each other. I'm too jealous."

Christy didn't even realize she felt these things. It amazed her to hear what was coming out of her mouth. "Did I just say that?"

"What, that you're jealous?"

"Yes."

"That's what you said. But do you want to know what I think? I think jealousy is normal when you love someone, and it's a good way to tell how much you care about him. The more jealous you get, the more you care."

Christy questioned whether that was true. After all, Katie had no experience in love. How would she know what's normal? Plus, when Todd quoted those verses on love, he had said that love was not jealous. She remembered that part.

"I don't know, Katie. All I know is that this Jasmine girl obviously means more to Todd than I do, and I must be pretty worthless if my competition is a girl in a wheelchair."

"Oh, low, Christy, low! I can't believe you said that. I don't think you're looking at this the right way. I mean, even if Todd had asked you, do you honestly think your parents would have let you go?"

"I don't know. Maybe. They treat him as if he's a long-lost nephew or something."

"I don't blame them! I'd treat Todd that way, too. He seems like the perfect guy."

"Yeah, well, maybe he's a little too perfect—a little too spiritual. He's always trying to see things from God's point of view, and it's too hard for me to catch up. I just don't think the way Todd does, or see things the way he does. Besides, weren't you the one who was telling me only a few days ago to let Todd go and move on, since Rick wanted to go to the prom with me?''

Katie wadded up her lunch bag, aimed, and made the shot into the trash can. She shook her head, her straight, red hair swinging like tassels.

"I don't know what I said then. But if you want my opinion now, I think Todd's worth trying to catch up to. I mean, wouldn't you rather be with a guy who's a few steps ahead of you emotionally or spiritually or whatever? Seems as though the few guys in my life have only been ahead of me physically, if you know what I mean.''

Christy smiled and nodded. She knew exactly what Katie meant.

"You do know, don't you,'' Katie said, leaning over and speaking in a hushed voice, "that a bunch of couples have rented hotel rooms at the Coronado for, you know, after the dance?''

"Are you kidding? People from our school?'' As soon as she said it, Christy realized she was being awfully naive. Of course other students at her school were doing stuff like that. She just never thought of who was doing what. She tended to think all her friends were innocent in the same way she was—except Alissa. And she certainly hadn't caught on until much later how intimately involved Alissa had been with her boyfriends.

"I heard that last year after the prom six of the guys on the football team and their dates were arrested for having a party in a hotel room. They were drunk and loud and smashed a bunch of furniture. The hotel security kicked them out.''

"That's disgusting,'' Christy said. "Why can't it be a nice, sweet innocent dance like, well, like in the movies?''

"I know,'' Katie said as the bell signaled the end of lunch. "I really hope another couple goes with us because, to be honest, I don't exactly know what Lance's idea of a good time is.''

Christy hurried to Spanish class, but Katie's final comment stayed with her. Would Lance really have a different idea from Katie's of what prom night should be? He did lean toward the dramatic, as the limo already represented. And Christy had learned enough to know that just because a guy said he was a Christian didn't mean he was operating out of the same value system that a deeply committed Christian would live by.

In a strange way, for the first time, Christy felt relieved that she wasn't going to the prom with Rick. Cheerleader tryouts presented enough pressure for one week, not to mention the algebra quiz.

The makeup quiz turned out to be harder than the first test. Christy handed it in and left class with a terrible headache. The last thing she wanted was to face Renee and be behind the rest of the girls who were trying out. If it hadn't been for Teri's offer to stay after to help, Christy probably would have given up the whole dream then and there.

"What are you doing here?" Renee said through clenched teeth as Christy slid into place right when a routine ended.

Teri turned to Renee and said, "You know what, Renee? The rest of us are getting sick of your comments. We're supposed to be building a team here. If you're so set on slamming somebody, why don't you slam me for being Mexican?"

"I would never do that, Teri!" Renee looked indignant. Her friends gathered around her, and Renee went on defending herself. "I'm not prejudiced against Hispanics or anybody!"

"Oh really? Then why are you against Christy just because she's a sophomore and the rest of us are juniors? It's the same thing as slamming me because the color of my skin is different from yours. I can't change my skin. Christy can't change her age.

You're the only one who can change, Renee. You can change your attitude."

Mrs. James stepped in and told the girls to sit down. They complied but spaced themselves out and took turns glancing at Renee, who sat with her arms crossed in front of her.

"I should have said something earlier," Mrs. James said with a concerned look. "I don't know what has gone on over the last few weeks of practice, but I can tell you what will go on during the next few days of practice and then once the team is formed. We will be a team: working together, looking out for each other, helping each other. Each of you will have equal value to me and to each other. Understand?"

The girls quietly nodded.

"There will be absolutely no more of these bad attitudes or cruel remarks. I don't know what all has been said, and I don't want to know, but I think now is the time for apologies. If any of you need to apologize to anyone else here, I'll wait and let you do that before we go into the next practice set."

No one moved. Christy searched her mind for something she could apologize for, but she saw herself as the victim who should be apologized to.

"Sorry," Teri said to the group. "I shouldn't have blown up like that. I apologize if I came on too strong, Renee."

Renee neither acknowledged Teri's apology nor offered hers to anyone.

"Okay," Mrs. James said, breaking the tension. "I can't make you apologize, but I will form this group into a team. Let's get going, and remember, I want you to work together on this."

They practiced the next routine for 20 minutes; then Mrs. James dismissed them. No one had much to say to anyone else. Christy stayed on the field with Teri, and they went right into the moves Christy had missed at the beginning of practice.

"Thanks for what you said, Teri. I really appreciated it," Christy said.

Teri batted her long braid of dark hair off her shoulder and shook her head. "I didn't say it very nicely."

"But you got the point across."

"Maybe. But if I didn't do it with love, it counts for nothing."

Christy froze. She had heard that phrase before. From Todd? "Is that in the Bible?"

"Yes, in First Corinthians."

"The Love Chapter," Christy added excitedly. "My boy—I mean, this guy I know said it to me last week. He's memorizing it. The whole chapter."

"Then he's a Christian?" Teri asked.

"Slightly! I mean, yes. So am I! Are you?"

"Yes!" Teri said, nodding enthusiastically.

The two gave each other a hug as if they had just found out they were related. Then, chattering quickly, Teri filled Christy in on the details of how she went to a church in which only Spanish was spoken and her dad was one of the pastors. With all the eager sharing between the two girls, they failed to get much practice in but decided to stay after on Wednesday and Thursday to help each other.

On her way home, Christy thought of how differently this day had ended than it had begun. She started by nearly losing Katie as her friend, and she ended with a new friend, Teri.

CHAPTER TEN

A Hollow Victory

Wednesday and Thursday flew by, and Christy improved a lot as Teri coached her. But Christy realized Teri was the better of the two of them. She had a certain grace and a vibrant smile that could be spotted halfway up the bleachers.

Christy's plan to beat out all the other girls had fueled her with angry energy for more than a week now. But getting so close to Teri made it hard, because she wouldn't want to make the team if Teri was the one who didn't.

It wasn't much of a prayer, but the only scrawny bit of communication Christy had with God on the day of tryouts was "Please let us both make it. Together we could be a much better witness for You."

She added the last part, thinking God might be more apt to do what she wanted if there was something in it for Him. Even as she thought the scrawny prayer, she realized how far she'd come from her original plan of honoring God by being on the cheerleading squad and being recognized on her campus as a God-lover. Right now she wasn't much of a vibrant testimony. She wasn't much of a vibrant anything.

The only thing she was being recognized for on her campus

was the girl who turned down Rick Doyle. Or more accurately, the girl who invited Rick to the prom and then turned around and canceled on him. It was awful to have so many people watching her and judging her by her actions.

Originally, that was what she thought would be the advantage of holding a position as a cheerleader. Now she detested the way people she didn't know came up to her and made strange comments about Rick. Many of them assumed she was a snob or at least extremely vengeful for what she had done to Rick. She didn't like the spotlight at all and determined that when she did make cheerleader, she'd be a quiet witness—a very quiet witness. That way people wouldn't expect so much from her.

The few times during the week that she saw Rick, he'd turned away or ignored her. She couldn't stand this tension and wished he would say something and get it over with. Christy wanted to say something and break the ice, if only she had an idea of what to say. Lately, it seemed that everything she'd done or said had soured. She didn't dare risk goofing things up with Rick even more than she had already.

Scholastically, Friday was a waste for Christy. She couldn't sit still or pay attention in any of her classes. She even moved her legs through the steps for her tryout routine under the desk in Spanish class. She couldn't eat a bite at lunch, so she searched the lunch area until she found Teri. Together they went to a quiet corner in the gym and went through the motions of their cheers, generously encouraging each other.

At last 3:00 came. Christy was the first one in the gym and the first one to put on the tryout uniform. She stood in front of the locker room mirror to admire the way the blue and gold stripes made each swish, each move, look sharper and more defined.

The other seven contestants filtered in soon after. By 3:15, Christy felt a current of electrical excitement crackling through the room as the girls briskly cuffed their socks and adjusted the ribbons they had been instructed to wear in their hair.

"Here, Christy," Teri offered, "try tucking your ribbon under your ponytail holder before tying it. Wait. I'll do it for you. That way it won't slip off while you're doing your routine."

"My hair never stays back on the sides," Christy nervously complained as Teri calmly tied the royal blue ribbon.

"Use more spray," Teri suggested. Her own hair looked perfect, curled tightly on the ends and held securely with a gold ribbon. "Here. Close your eyes. I'll do it."

Teri sprayed and tucked and fussed with Christy's hair before announcing, "There. It looks perfect, and believe me, it'll stay in place now."

Christy opened her eyes and saw how much better her hair looked after Teri's loving touch. She also saw Renee. Renee's dark hair was set off by both a gold and a blue ribbon.

"Why are you helping her?" Renee asked Teri.

Teri didn't look up. She calmly tucked her brush and hair spray back into her bag and said, "You don't want to know."

"What do you mean, I don't want to know. I asked, didn't I? Why are you helping her?"

Christy was amazed at Teri's strength and confidence and the way she held her ground with Renee.

"I'll tell you why, but you won't want to hear it."

"Why?" Renee challenged, her hand on her hip.

"Because it's the same reason I told you last year after tryouts when you asked if I was mad that you made it and I didn't."

"Oh." Renee looked bothered. "You mean that stuff about being a church girl."

Christy watched the two girls' reflections in the mirror as they faced each other. Teri's face looked soft and kind, while Renee's looked hard and angry.

"It's not that I'm a church girl, Renee. It's that I love God. And His Word says that if I love Him, I'm supposed to love my neighbor as much as I love myself."

Renee had no answer. Only a slight flinching look on her face. Then snapping out of their conversation, she shouted to all the girls, "Let's go! We're supposed to be on the floor at 3:30 exactly. That's right now!"

With a few last glances into the mirror, the girls lined up and filed as calmly as possible into the gym. Mrs. James handed each of them a small numbered paper circle to pin on the front of their uniforms and pointed to the eight chairs before them, each with corresponding numbers.

As Christy found her chair, number four, she took a quick survey of the partially filled bleachers. In an instant, she spotted her mom. She flashed her mother a forced, nervous smile. It was nice of her to come. Christy hadn't expected it. It meant her mom was taking time off work to be here for her. That knowledge made Christy feel special.

Still smiling, trying to look energetic and confident, Christy scanned the row of judges. None of them smiled back.

"Number one," a judge called, and the first contestant stood.

Wouldn't you know it would be Renee, Christy thought.

When the signal was given, Renee rallied out to the center of the gym, giving it all she had. She was good. On the outside, she had exactly what it took to be a great cheerleader.

Number two was called, and Christy felt her stomach doing cartwheels.

What if I forget everything? What if I fall flat on my face? What if—

Her thoughts were interrupted by a tap on her shoulder. Someone she didn't know handed her a slip of paper and then hurried away. She glanced down at the note: "Go for it, Killer. I'm with you all the way."

Rick?

She looked around but didn't see him. She had managed to avoid contact with him all week and wasn't sure that even if she did spot him at this moment, she would want to make eye contact.

What does this mean? she thought. *That he's not mad about the prom anymore?*

The judge called, "Number three," and Christy thought, *Actually, he has been supportive of me all through this cheerleader thing. We did agree to be friends no matter what. He must understand about my parents' rules and everything. I feel so relieved!*

Christy decided it was a good thing, too, that she suddenly felt so relieved, because suddenly number four was called. With gusto and a bright enthusiasm that made her stand out from the others, Christy rushed to the center of the floor.

> Stand back, watch out
> You're up against the best
> Cougars, uh-huh, a step above the rest!
> You'd better back off
> We're hot on your trail
> The KHS Cougars will never fail!

Breathing hard and shivering with excitement, Christy jogged back to her seat. She felt as if every nerve inside her was quivering. *I did it! I did it!*

It took every bit of composure to settle calmly into her seat and stay there. Christy knew she had done her best. She was cheerleader material. After that performance, there couldn't be any doubt from anyone. Not from her own opinion of herself. Not from Rick. Not even from Renee. She'd proved herself to all of them, just as she'd planned.

Christy scanned the bleacher rows for Rick. Her mom caught her eye and waved, offering Christy a big smile. After returning the smile, Christy kept searching for Rick.

Where is he?

Leaning back slightly in her chair, she tried to see if he was behind her. Instead, her gaze met Teri's. What an energetic, encouraging smile!

Teri mouthed the word "Perfect," and Christy felt showered with the warmth of her friend's praise.

Teri really knows how to show people that she loves them. I'd like to be more like that.

Christy gave up trying to find Rick. She focused her concentration on numbers five and six. Inwardly, she began to cheer for Teri. *Come on, Teri. I know you can do it.*

The next two girls did very well, and then came one of Renee's friends. Christy didn't think that much of her routine, but then she didn't think much of the girl either. When she was only one eight-count into the cheer, this girl messed up and had to ask the judges if she could start over.

Christy tried to feel sympathy for Renee's friend, but she actually felt glad to see her lose points. That gave Teri an advantage, and she needed it. Poor Teri had number eight, the worst slot to have, the last contestant.

At last number eight was called, and Teri sprang onto the floor. *Come on, Teri!*

Christy knew Teri would be the best of all of them. Not just because Teri knew the routine so well, but because Christy had seen how Teri stood up to Renee and wasn't afraid to tell people about her relationship with God. Of course God would let Teri become a cheerleader—especially since she didn't make it last year. She'd be the vibrant living testimony Christy had once thought she could be for their whole school.

Teri did a toe touch, something she did better than anyone else. But somehow she came down off balance and fell awkwardly. She sprawled on the gym floor as the spectators gasped. Managing to pull herself up, she finished the routine as best she could, but it turned out weak and sloppy and minus two important jumps. Not Teri's usual style at all.

The observers clapped the loudest for Teri as she awkwardly hobbled back to her chair. Christy could see tears streaming down her cheeks. With dignity, Teri lowered herself to her chair and waited with the others, even though it was obvious that she was in pain.

Christy wanted to rush over and do something. The adviser quietly spoke to Teri and handed her a bag of ice, which Teri calmly placed against her ankle and waited for the next part of the tryouts.

The judges finished their scoring and then called the contestants back out to the center of the gym floor. The final part of tryouts was the easiest. The girls had to perform a short cheer together so the judges could see how they worked as a squad.

Springing from their seats, clapping, cheering, their skirts swishing, the girls rushed into formation. Christy ran with the others, clapping and smiling. That's when she noticed that Teri was missing. She hadn't come out on the floor with them.

Christy glanced over at Teri, sitting alone holding the ice on her ankle, the tears still glistening on her cheeks.

That was it. The decision had been made, they all knew it. Since Teri didn't compete in this event, she wouldn't qualify, and the seven girls who now stood on the gym floor would be next year's cheerleaders.

They ran back to their seats after the routine, giving each other looks of triumph, knowing the cut had been made, and it wasn't one of them. They couldn't let their assumptions be known because they'd been instructed to control their responses.

Christy wondered why the judges didn't go ahead and say something. It was an unusual year in that never before had so few tried out for the squad. Usually, a dozen girls competed. The only reason Christy could imagine the judges remaining silent about the winners was that Kelley High had an old tradition that the announcement of who made the squad wasn't posted or made public to the school until at least a week after tryouts. It was the same way with the sports teams as well.

Mrs. James had once said the reason was to allow the teachers to agree on the involvement of the students in the sport or activity and make sure there was no conflict with conduct or grades. This year the big announcement would be no surprise. All the students and parents who had come to tryouts knew they were looking at the chosen seven.

Christy couldn't stop smiling. She was going to be a cheerleader! Why, oh why didn't they break their tradition for this year only and announce the names of the winners right now? What good was it to know and be so excited when you couldn't let out a squeal of delight?

With tryouts officially over, the girls were dismissed. Noisy feet stampeded down the bleachers. Christy ran off the floor and into the locker room, looking for Teri. She found her in the coach's office, her foot covered with a large bag of ice and propped up on a chair. The tears had smeared her makeup, and Teri looked pitiful.

"You okay?" Christy asked softly, her emotions leaping every time she thought of her victory, then instantly crashing when she thought of Teri. It was a terrible combination of feelings to have to endure in the same moment.

"No, but I will be." Teri's voice quivered. Then with a strength and dignity that Christy knew she never could have at such a moment, Teri said, "Congratulations, Christy! I'm so glad you made the squad!"

Christy could tell that she really meant it, too.

"I feel awful," Christy began.

"Don't! You should be very proud of yourself. You did a great job. The best I've ever seen you do!"

"I wouldn't have if you hadn't helped me. I hope you know that. I just feel so bad for you, Teri."

Christy's mom walked in at that moment and looked at Teri. "Are you all right, dear?"

Teri nodded.

Turning to Christy, Mom said, "Christy, I must say, I didn't even know you were my own daughter out there. You did an excellent job!"

"Thanks, Mom." Christy smiled weakly. This is what she had wanted all along: the recognition, the praise, and the affirmation from her friends and family. But hearing it in front of Teri turned the victory into a hollow pleasure. How could she enjoy her dream when the one who helped make it come true had just lost hers?

"Do you want to go home with me now, or spend some time with all your friends back in the gym?" Mom asked.

"I'd rather go now. Bye, Teri." Christy gave her a gentle hug. "I'll see you Monday. Take care of your foot, okay?"

Teri forced a smile. "I will. Thanks."

Christy and her mom stepped out of the office and nearly ran into a giddy, flying Renee. Even the sight of Christy didn't diminish her enthusiasm.

"Oh, hi!" she squeaked. "I guess you're officially one of us now, huh? Well, congratulations, and I'm sure you'll be a great addition to our team."

Is it because my mom's right here that she's being this sweet? Is it because of what Mrs. James has been saying all week about being a team? Or is it because the pressure is off and she knows she made the squad so there's no doubt that she'll be head cheerleader?

"Thanks," Christy returned cordially but not as sweetly. "And congratulations to you, too, Renee."

Renee's face looked bright and zingy as she cheerfully retorted, "Was there any doubt that I'd make it?"

Christy excused herself so she could change out of the uniform and leave with her mom before Renee decided to continue gushing all over them.

"Let's stop and get some ice cream to celebrate," Mom suggested on the way home. "Your dad will be so proud of you. I wish he could have seen you. Why, Christy, I never would have guessed that you had this side of you! You were very, very good out there."

Christy should have been excited and ready to celebrate, but inside she felt dismal and small. *You'd be surprised, Mom, how much you don't know about the real me. Nobody does. Except maybe God. But what kind of a God would let Teri hurt her foot knowing how much I need her to be on the squad with me?*

Heavy questions weighed Christy down all weekend. On the outside, she responded the way everyone wanted her to: happy and excited and proud that she had made the squad. Aunt Marti and Uncle Bob even called Friday night and promised to come see her at as many games as they could. Marti insisted on paying for Christy's entire outfit, no matter how much it cost. That relief of the financial pressure alone should have sent Christy's emotions soaring. However, on the inside she had never felt so lonely.

Saturday night, prom night, Christy talked her mom into renting a movie, and the two of them sat on the couch, watching *The Man from Snowy River*. Mom cried during some parts; Christy cried all the way through. The piano music that Jessica, the girl in the movie, played when she brooded over her boyfriend haunted Christy.

She couldn't fall asleep that night. *I wonder if Katie is having the time of her life? I wonder if the dress she borrowed worked out okay? Who did Rick go with? Did he think of me at all? Why didn't he call me after he sent that note to me at tryouts? Was he even there? I never saw him. I wish I knew what he was thinking.*

Then, because she couldn't help her thoughts from taking her to the next turn in the winding path of her remorse, Christy wondered about Todd. *He's probably not thinking of me at all, now that he has Jasmine. I wonder if he's going to kiss her tonight. Has he kissed her before? The kisses he's given me can't be all that special if he's also kissing other girls.*

Then a sharp, painful realization hit Christy deep in her heart. *I've kissed another guy. I've kissed Rick. Todd doesn't know. If he did, would he think the times I've kissed him were less special? I wish I'd never kissed Rick, or more accurately, I wish I'd never let Rick kiss me. And I wish I'd never kissed Todd. I wish I'd never kissed either of them!*

Christy felt tears coming to her eyes in the darkness of her bedroom and in the darkness of her heart. *No, I don't mean that. I don't wish I'd never kissed Todd. I only wish it didn't hurt so much now.*

I wish I didn't care about him so much. I have to stop these feelings from growing. Bury them even deeper. It won't hurt so much if I don't care so much. Come on. I managed to hide my frustration with Renee. I can hide these feelings, too.

Christy was exhausted by Sunday morning, having wrestled all night with herself. She turned especially moody when she arrived at the toddlers' class and found out Katie wasn't there.

Christy couldn't believe how heavily this sadness hung on her shoulders. It didn't matter one bit that she had made the cheerleading squad. She still felt empty and all alone. And that bothered her. Christy assumed that once she became a cheerleader, all those stressful feelings would go away and she would feel good and satisfied and energetic all the time.

Not so.

And she couldn't bury all her feelings about Todd. Nor could she hide the depression she felt over the fact that Katie went to the prom without her. She felt melancholy as she passed out Play-Doh to the toddlers.

"Here you go," she said, handing Ashley a lump of the dough.

"Make something fo' me, Cwissy," Ashley said, her blue, button eyes looking up expectantly.

"Okay." Christy pulled up a low chair next to Ashley. "What do you want me to make?"

"I dunno."

"Here," Christy quickly rolled out a long line, then held it up for Ashley. "It's a snake!"

"Eeeee!" Ashley squealed. "I don't want a snake."

"Look, Teacher," one boy said. "I made a snake, too." He dangled it in front of Ashley, and she appropriately squealed again.

"Okay, okay," Christy said, squashing the green, gushy stuff in the palm of her hand so that it squeezed out through her fingers. "We can make anything you want, Ashley. Here, you squash some, too."

A waterfall of thoughts cascaded through Christy's mind as she pressed the warmed clay into her hand. She had told Rick once that he made her feel like Play-Doh. Was he, like Katie had said, still interested in trying to make her into what he wanted her to be, like a pliable plaything?

And then another Todd thought crashed over the rocky places of her mind: *Soft hearts are the only kind that God can hold in His hand and mold.*

"Storytime," the teacher called, and some of the children scrambled over to the rug while a few slowpokes tried to finish up their projects. Christy helped scoot them along and then got the snack ready, half listening to the story.

The teacher began to tell about Jonathan and David when a little girl interrupted her. "My friend has twin brothers, and their names are Jonathan and David."

"This is a different Jonathan and David," the teacher explained with a smile. "These boys lived a long, long time ago, in Bible times. They were very good friends, and they both loved God. Jonathan's father was the king."

"My friend has a dog named King," a little boy said.

"Let's listen to the story now," the teacher continued patiently.

I could never teach a bunch of interrupters like these kids are, Christy thought. *I'd never have the patience.*

"Now, Jonathan deserved to be the next king because he was the king's son. But do you know what? God wanted David to be king, and Jonathan knew it. Did Jonathan fight with David and say, 'I deserve to be king. Get out of my way!'?"

All the toddlers shook their heads and said, "Noooo."

"That's right. Jonathan loved David, and he helped him become the next king, because Jonathan knew that God wanted David to be king and not him. Do you know what the Bible says love is?"

Christy stood perfectly still, waiting for what the teacher would say, not for the toddlers' benefit but for hers.

From memory the teacher quoted part of the Love Chapter. "Love is patient, love is kind, and is not jealous . . ."

Christy shut it all out. Not those verses again! She didn't need another reminder of Todd. Not now. Quietly humming the piano music from the movie, she ignored the rest of the story.

CHAPTER ELEVEN

I Can Wait

Christy walked alone into the church service. None of her friends had showed up; they were probably all too tired from the prom. The loneliness she had felt for several days now throbbed within her. She found her parents and sat with them, which felt safe and comforting.

She tried to put a lot into the service, singing and following along with her Bible during the sermon. She even underlined a verse or two.

Oddly, the thought that kept pounding to the front of her mind was a line from the teacher's story to the toddlers. "God wanted David to be king, and Jonathan knew it." She didn't know what to make of this thought that refused to go away.

That afternoon while everyone at her house took a nap, Christy reread a letter that came the day before from her friend Paula. Paula and Christy had been best friends since they were toddlers, but Paula still lived in their hometown in Wisconsin.

Paula's correspondence tended to be short and written with large, curvy letters with tiny hearts instead of dots over the i's. She wrote about guys. Several guys. Guys Christy had never met. It all seemed so far away. Like another lifetime.

Paula wrote at least once a month, and in every letter she talked about how she was saving money to come out to see Christy that summer. At first Christy wanted nothing more than to have Paula come and be part of her new life in California. Yet, as the year wore on, Paula seemed more and more like a stranger.

Christy knew she should write Paula back and tell her about the cheerleading victory and all. But after 10 minutes of doodling on a piece of notebook paper, Christy gave up and called Katie instead.

She was actually a little mad at Katie for not calling her first and giving her all the details. Christy punched in Katie's phone number and tried to coach herself to sound positive when Katie answered the phone.

"Well? Tell me everything. Did you have fun?"

Katie paused before saying, "I guess. It was all right."

"All right! That's all you can say? It was all right?"

"Yeah, it was all right. I don't think you missed much."

"Katie, what happened?"

"Nothing. That's just it. Here I had this big dream about what the prom would be like, but it wasn't like I thought it would be at all."

"You mean you didn't have fun being with Lance? He's usually the life of the party."

"Exactly! And that's why it turned out the way it did. Mr. Life-of-the-Party took off and ignored me the whole time. We danced only once for half a dance, and that was because I made him. The rest of the time I just sat there, watching everybody else."

Christy didn't know what to say. She searched for some possible positive points. "Well, did he give you flowers?"

"Yeah." Katie laughed, but it wasn't a happy remembrance

kind of laugh. "He gave me a corsage. A huge corsage that didn't match my dress at all. I told him my dress was blue. He said he forgot. The flowers were green. Green, Christy! You know how they spray-paint white carnations? Well, these were painted green and looked like some leftover bargain from St. Patrick's Day."

Christy laughed and sympathized at the same time. "How awful!"

"Oh, that's not the worst of it," Katie said, warming up. "You know my dress? The one I borrowed from Janelle? Well, you never saw it, but there's no place to pin a corsage. Especially when my corsage was a head of lettuce."

They both laughed.

"I carried it around all night. In the box. I felt as though I were carrying around a cafeteria tray! Oh, and the food—oh, man, we're talking major mystery meat. They poured some creamy mushroom sauce over it, but nobody ate it. I ate some of my salad, and that's all. I hadn't eaten anything all day, and I was starving!"

"Sounds as though you could have nibbled on your corsage if you got real hungry," Christy teased.

"I thought about it, believe me!"

"So, what else happened? Did you go with Rick and his date?"

"No. Rick didn't go. I didn't see him there at all. Nobody said anything. I don't know what's going on with him."

"That's strange. I wonder why he didn't go," Christy said.

"Who knows. Oh, you want to hear the worst part? After my mom got all excited about my going, she decided I had to be home by midnight. Can you believe it? We had this big fight about my curfew right before Lance came. Then he got there, and my mom took all these stupid pictures. I didn't smile in any of them."

"Katie!"

"I was so mad. It didn't help when Lance came in wearing, get this, a white tux with tails, a black top hat and—are you ready?— orange high tops!"

"No!"

"Yes!"

"What a nerd!"

"Not Lance. He turned out to be the life of the party, like I said. He must have danced with half the girls there, and he had his picture taken with at least a dozen of them. They all wanted the nice formal picture with their dates, then a wild and crazy one with Lance."

"That's incredible. I can't believe this happened to you, Katie!" Christy tried to sound sympathetic; yet she couldn't help feeling relieved that she hadn't gone through the same embarrassing experience.

"I haven't even told you the worst part. When I told Lance I had to be home at midnight, I was totally humiliated. Then, when it was 11:30, I had to interrupt him while he was dancing with Renee."

"Oh, of all people! She'll never let you forget it either."

"So, get this; Lance walks me to the limo and tells the driver to take me home and then come back for him."

"No!" Christy tried to muffle her scream so she wouldn't wake her napping family. "That's awful!"

"Tell me about it!"

"What did you do?"

"I ate half the food in the refrigerator and watched TV."

"You mean when you got home?"

"No, in the limo. They had a refrigerator and TV in the limo."

"You're kidding! There was a refrigerator and a TV in the limo?"

"Yep. It was the only highlight of my pathetic evening, believe me."

"What a riot!" Christy said.

"I'm glad you think so. That was one evening I hope I never have to repeat. And since I asked him to the prom, I was the one who paid for the tickets! What a joke, huh? I don't want to go to school tomorrow. I don't think I can show my face around that crowd ever again."

"Oh Katie, it won't be that bad. Renee has been torturing me for a couple of weeks now, and I've survived. You'll bounce back. You always do."

"I don't know. I just wish you would have gone. You and I would have had fun together, even if both our dates turned out to be jerks."

Christy wondered if Rick would have turned out to be such a jerk, spending the whole time flirting with all the other girls. She told Katie about the note she got at tryouts.

"If you want my opinion, I think Rick has it set in his mind that one day he's going to marry you."

"Oh come on, Katie! Why would you even say that?"

"His parents are pretty strict. Did you know that? I think he likes you because you're so young, sweet, innocent, and all that. He flirts with all the wild girls at church and school, but he probably figures that you're the kind of girl his parents would approve of."

As usual, Katie's comments gave Christy something to think about. After hanging up, she went outside and sat on the front step. It was a cool afternoon with thin clouds veiling the blue sky. The fragrance of the jasmine was faint under the trellis. The neighborhood was quiet except for the sound of a lawn mower in the distance.

For a while Christy hummed the piano music from the movie and thought about Katie, Lance, Rick, and Todd. For some strange reason, the time she spent sympathizing with Katie on the phone helped to soften the hurts she'd been feeling. At least she had some good things to look forward to when she went back to school tomorrow. She would be identified as a cheerleader, even though the announcement wasn't yet official. Still, everyone would know. And they would look at her differently.

Then all of a sudden the line from Sunday school pushed all the other thoughts aside and marched boldly before her: "God wanted David to be king, and Jonathan knew it." It was beginning to bug her. That one line was like a line from a commercial that kept coming back even when she tried hard to forget it.

"Was does that mean? Why do I keep thinking of that one line?" she asked aloud, and as she spoke the words, she realized she was talking to God the way she used to—openly and easily.

Christy knew the time had come to stop ignoring God and to get everything out in the open. She didn't like being cut off and isolated from God the way she'd been. It was like a bumper sticker she once saw that said, "If you feel far from God, guess who moved?"

It wasn't hard to admit that she'd been the one who'd moved away from God. She was the one ignoring Him, and it had only made her feel lonely and miserable.

"I'm sorry, Lord. I've been doing everything without You. I can tell, because even though I got what I wanted, the cheerleading and all, well, I feel so lonely. I know it's because I haven't spent any time with You. I'm sorry."

She felt relieved. Not as though all her burdens had been

lifted or anything like that. All her problems were still there. But now she didn't feel that she was all alone in trying to figure things out.

She began with Todd. "What am I supposed to do with my relationship with Todd?" There was no answer—only the calm afternoon breeze dancing through the jasmine, sending the flower's perfume into the air.

Love is patient, Christy found herself thinking. She took it into her heart and held it a moment before telling herself, "You need to be more patient. The relationship isn't over yet. You're the one who tried to bury it, not Todd. You need to wait and see what happens, Christy."

Not exactly a settling conclusion, but one she could live with. She knew deep down that she needed to be fair with Todd and let go of the jealousy that had eaten a hole in her pride.

After all, she reasoned, *I've been able to be friends with Rick, but it's not in the same way that I'm friends with Todd. So why can't Todd be good friends with Jasmine and still be close to me?*

Then she thought about Rick. *What am I supposed to do about him?* No answer came on the wind. No clear thought paraded through her mind.

Something still nagged her. It wasn't Todd or Rick. Something else, but she couldn't figure out what.

Am I doing something wrong, God? I really want to do what's right. I want to make You happy.

The only thing she could think of was cheerleading. But what was wrong with that? She had made the squad; she had gotten past the point where Renee seriously bothered her, and she had made a good friend, Teri.

Teri. I wish she had made the squad. She's better than I am, and I know it. She's a stronger Christian, too. And it's going to be her senior year next year. I wish there were some way Teri could be on the squad.

Christy pulled a flower from the trellis and plucked its petals. She still wasn't certain what was bothering her. She would try to get it out by writing in her diary.

Stretching out on her bed, Christy found a fresh page to write on. She opened up to her last entry from almost two weeks ago and read about her desire to become a cheerleader for God, but above all, to pursue her cheerleading dream in such a way that she would be a good example of a Christian.

"I didn't really do it for You, did I?" Christy whispered into the stillness. "I did it for myself, and it didn't make me a whole lot more like You. It kind of made me more like Renee and the others."

Now, with devout determination, she penned, *I'm going to do it for You now, Lord. I'm going to let all the girls on the squad know that I'm a Christian. I'm going to be a good example of You to them and the whole school.*

Such a sincere vow should have eased Christy's heart considerably. It didn't. She still felt a strange nagging. It persisted all evening, so before she went to bed she knelt beside her bed and said, "I still feel as though something is wrong between us, God, but I don't know what it is." She paused. "Will You please show me what it is and what I should do to make it right, whatever it is that's bugging me? Thanks, Father. Good night."

Christy wondered if she was trying to make things right with God the way she'd tried to make things right with her mom when she forgot to put the towels in the dryer. Even though she knew that wasn't the way God wanted her to approach her relationship with Him, it still seemed it would help smooth things over for the way she'd ignored Him for so long.

When she got up at 7:00, Christy felt as if she hadn't slept at all, which made her even more exhausted than she'd been the day before.

She bustled around her room, getting ready, and bumped into her dresser, giving herself a huge black and blue mark on her hip.

Katie said her morning had gone about the same when the girls met at their lockers. They decided to be miserable together all day.

That proved difficult for Christy. She kept receiving congratulations from people she didn't even know, and then at lunch, Rick came looking for her. She could tell he was looking for her by the way he walked toward her with his eyes set in her direction.

"Hey, Killer!" he called while still a few yards away. A couple of people looked to see whom Rick was talking to. Christy could almost hear their whispered answers: "Oh, look! That's the new cheerleader."

Christy stared at her half-eaten orange. This wasn't her. She didn't like the attention. She didn't want people watching her, breaking through her invisible wall of privacy.

"Hey, Killer," Rick said again, now standing right behind her, his hand on her shoulder. He squatted down to be more on eye level with her.

She turned around to look at him, fully aware that they had an audience.

"Come here," he said, motioning with his head. "I reserved a place for two over there."

Gathering her things, Christy followed him. She felt like a puppy on a leash. She knew people were talking about them. Rick led her over to "their" wall, where they had sat when he had given her the pep talk about hanging in there with the cheerleading tryouts. Rick planted himself on the wall. Christy remained standing, hugging her notebook in front of her like a shield. She had no reason to fear Rick; yet she felt insecure and timid.

"So, how's my favorite Rah-Rah? Didn't I tell you, you would make it? You were perfect. Absolutely perfect. I looked for you afterward to tell you, but you'd disappeared. Did you get my note?" He smiled at her, his deep brown eyes melting her.

"Yes. Thanks for all your encouragement. I probably wouldn't have made it without you."

"I told you, you'd make it! I would have been really disappointed in you if you had quit. You deserved to make it. You know, I feel as though you and I are more on the same level now."

Christy wasn't sure how to take that. "You mean I wasn't good enough for you before?" she taunted.

Rick smiled his half smile. "Let's just say that now you're more my kind of girl."

The way he said it she couldn't tell if he was teasing or serious. In any case she felt uncomfortable. The thought of being "good enough" for Rick disgusted her.

What a shallow value system you must have, she thought. *All on the outside for show. What about the real me on the inside? Doesn't that matter to you? Katie was right. You are just trying to shape me into the perfect girlfriend.*

"So," Rick said, changing the subject, "Katie said you canceled going to the prom with me because of your parents."

Christy paused a moment, debating how to best respond. She knew honesty was always the best way. At least that's what she'd tried to tell her little brother. Maybe she needed to take her own advice. "Well, to be honest with you, Rick, my parents never said I could go in the first place. I just hoped they would, and so I went ahead and made plans. But then they said no. Actually, they said it a lot stronger than that because they're not at all in favor of dances or proms or any of that. So that's why I had to cancel on you."

Christy remembered the hurt she felt when Rick hung up on her. She wanted him to apologize and hinted by saying, "I'm sorry things worked out the way they did. As I told you on the phone that day, I'm really sorry."

"Don't worry about it," Rick said, without apologizing for his part of the hurt. "I still have first take on your birthday. I even wrote it on my calendar. July 27th. It will be a night you'll never forget."

First take! Who am I that you think you can push me into any shape you want? Maybe I don't want to go out with you ever! And why couldn't you apologize for hanging up on me? You're too proud to say you're sorry, that's your problem, Rick Doyle!

Months ago when Rick asked if he could take her out on her sixteenth birthday, she had blushed and felt honored. Now she wanted to push him off the wall for his cockiness. *Oh, if only I had the nerve to say those things to him!* She swallowed all of it and said absolutely nothing.

Rick swung his legs back and forth, kicking his heels against the bricks. "Did you hear much about the prom?" he asked. "From what I hear, we didn't miss much."

"Why didn't you go?" Christy blurted out. It came out like an accusation.

Rick looked surprised. "What was the point if I couldn't go with you?"

Christy gave him her best let's-get-real look and said, "Why don't you just tell me the truth?"

He fumbled around with a few meaningless words before looking over his shoulder and saying, "Okay, I can tell you, Christy. Actually, you're the one I should be telling." He rounded his shoulders and said quietly, "My parents didn't want me to go."

"Rick, there's nothing shameful about that. If you remember, that's why I didn't go either."

"I know. But there's more," Rick continued. "Mine said they weren't in favor of it, but if I was determined to go, they didn't want me to go behind their backs. They said I could go only with a Christian girl, preferably someone from church. And I had to pay for it myself."

"So, why didn't you go with one of the girls at church?"

He looked at her as if she had asked a stupid question.

"Because none of them are my kind of girl. You know, the Rah-Rah type. And besides, do you know how much it costs? By the time I rented a tux and bought flowers and everything, it'd be half my life savings. For that kind of money, I wouldn't show up with some girl who would be off with her friends all night."

It all made sense. Rick's personality became transparent to Christy as he spoke. Katie had been so right. He did want to make Christy into "his kind of girl": someone who had all the right qualifications on the outside; a girl who would give him undivided attention and follow him around, shy and quiet, letting him be the star.

"You know, Rick . . ." Christy felt her heart thumping as she spoke up. "I'm not so sure I am your kind of girl."

"Sure you are! Or at least you're going to be. You've come a long way, Christy. I can wait until you get it all together."

"Okay, then let me rephrase that. I'm not so sure that you're my kind of guy. You see, I want someone who's patient and kind and not jealous. A guy who knows that what's on the inside is more important than what's on the outside. And I just don't see you being that kind of guy."

Rick looked shocked at her truthful words. "You don't see me as that kind of guy?"

"No," Christy said bravely. "But you could be." And then for flair she added, "And I can wait."

Christy turned and walked off fast and strong, with her heart pounding wildly.

CHAPTER TWELVE

A Laurel Crown

"That's on Friday afternoon, as in tomorrow, not next week," added Christy's history teacher while reading the announcement, "an all-school assembly will be held in the auditorium at 2:00. Next year's football team will be presented, and next year's cheer-leaders will be announced."

"As if we don't already know who the cheerleaders are," said a girl in the front row.

Christy could feel the gaze of her classmates on her. She kept looking straight ahead.

"Open your books to chapter 17, and since I'm sure you all read this last night, as I asked you to, I'd like you to spend the rest of class answering the review questions at the end of this sec-tion."

The usual groans and shuffling of books ensued, and Christy hurried to get going on the assignment. She already had plenty of homework and didn't want any more. Unfortunately, she made it through only half the questions before the teacher announced that whatever they didn't finish in class would be due tomorrow, and they also needed to read chapter 18. Now it was Christy's turn to groan and shuffle her books.

"Seems as though all the teachers are piling it on now that school is almost over," said a guy next to Christy as they left the classroom.

"I know," Christy groaned.

"I think they want to cram everything in so they can put it all on our finals."

"I'm not looking forward to that," Christy commented, inching her way down the crowded hall with the guy. She didn't even know his name, and he hadn't spoken to her all year. It seemed a little odd that he'd suddenly turned so friendly. Just then Christy spotted Teri standing by her locker.

"Excuse me," she said. "I want to see how Teri is doing."

"Yeah," the guy said quickly, "too bad about her foot. Glad you made cheerleader, though. Congratulations!"

So that's it! He's suddenly paying attention to me because I'm going to be a cheerleader. How shallow can people be? Christy thought in disgust.

"No crutches?" she asked Teri, coming up alongside her.

"No," Teri said. "I hobbled around this weekend, but it's fine now."

"That's good news," Christy said.

"Yes, well, the real good news is going to be tomorrow," Teri said without a hint of jealousy. "I know how much you wanted to be a cheerleader, Christy, and I'm really glad you made it."

"It hasn't been announced yet, Teri."

"No, but everybody knows who got it. It's not going to be a surprise this year. I mean it's obvious, don't you think?"

"Aren't you even upset about it? You worked so hard, and you're so good, and it's going to be your senior year and everything. Aren't you even a little hurt or angry?"

Teri smiled her dazzling smile and said, "Kind of. You know,

I really thought that's what God wanted me to do—be a cheer-leader next year. But I guess I was wrong."

The bell clanged loudly above their heads. Teri squeezed Christy's arm before slipping into her classroom and said, "I'm going to be in the front row tomorrow, cheering my heart out for you, Christy."

At that instant, it was as if a loud bell had gone off inside of Christy's heart, and suddenly she knew what she had to do. It was suddenly completely clear.

Katie came looking for Christy after school at her locker. "Where were you at lunch?"

"Oh, I had to talk to somebody."

"Who? Rick?" Katie prodded.

"No, Mrs. James. About some cheerleader stuff."

"Are you getting excited about the assembly tomorrow?"

"I guess." Christy shrugged and tried to smile at Katie.

"Well, this is your first year here, so maybe you don't realize what a big deal they make of this at Kelley High. The athlete of the year calls the girls' names, and they run onto the stage and line up in front of the football players. They always start crying. It's a big deal. Better wear waterproof mascara tomorrow."

"Okay," Christy said.

"Did I tell you who made mascot for next year? It's supposed to be a secret until they announce it at assembly tomorrow, but of course they told me because they wanted to know if my cougar mascot outfit from last year would fit him."

"Him?"

"Clifford Weed! Can you believe it?"

"I don't think I know him."

"He's huge! He'll make a great cougar. But they'll have to come up with a new cougar suit."

"Are you kind of sad that your year as mascot is already over?"

"Not really," Katie said. Then she quickly added, "Well, kind of, I guess. It's funny how it always ends up being different from what you think it's going to be."

"Like the prom?" Christy ventured.

"Don't go there, Christy."

Christy pulled her algebra book from her locker and crammed it into her already-filled backpack.

"Do you want to come over this afternoon?" Katie asked.

"I've got so much homework," Christy complained. "I need to get going on it. I want to get it all done during the week, because my mom said Todd called last night after I'd already gone to sleep, and he's coming down this weekend."

"So you guys are back together?"

"Oh, I don't know."

"What? Aren't you anxious to see him?"

"Yes and no. I want to see him and spend time with him and get things settled and back to normal with our relationship, but I'm not ready to hear about his prom and Jasmine and all that."

"Well, if you ask me, after going to the prom with Lance, I can sincerely tell you that whatever it takes to hold on to a guy like Todd, well, honey, JDI."

"What?"

"You know, JDI—'Just do it.' You've got to give it your best shot and don't ever give up! There are too many Lances in this world and not enough Todds."

"You know what amazes me, Katie?"

"What?"

"Sometimes you are so right!"

"Only sometimes?"

They both laughed, and Christy said, "Yes, only sometimes.

And that's because you change your opinions faster than anyone I know. First you say I should go for Rick; then you say I should hold on to Todd. Make up your mind."

Katie tilted her head and said, "Make up my mind? Why? It doesn't matter what I think, ultimately, does it? I mean, aren't you the one who should make up your mind and stick to what you believe and what you want?"

Even though Katie's words were offered lightheartedly, they stung. Christy knew she had a problem with making decisions. It made her wonder if some of the decisions she'd made the last few days were ones she'd regret later.

"As I said, Katie, sometimes you are so right. I do have to improve at making my own decisions and sticking with them no matter what."

"But Christy . . ." Katie's voice and expression turned soft and understanding. "Don't you think you've done about the best you could lately with all the stuff that's been thrown at you?"

"I don't know."

"Well, if you want my opinion—and remember, this is only my opinion—you have to decide this for yourself. But I think you've done just fine. Look how everything turned out. You made the cheerleading squad, you made your point with Rick so he doesn't think he can run your life, and you're going to see Todd and pick up where you left off with him. I think that, for all that's happened, you've done just fine."

Christy gave her pal an appreciative hug. "Do you know what the best thing is about going to school every day?"

"No, I have no idea what could be the best thing about going to school. Believe me." Katie's eyes were full of mischief.

"It's that I always know you're going to be here for me."

Katie smiled.

"Thank you. I feel the same way," Katie said. "I always know you'll be there for me, too."

"Even when I goof up on prom plans?" Christy said.

"Oh, hey! That's what keeps life interesting. Think how boring life would be if everything always went the way we planned it. Believe me, I've learned that sometimes the best answers to prayers are the ones God doesn't answer."

"What?"

"You think about that for a while. Think about how often we change our minds. If God gave us everything we asked for, we'd be in chaos."

Christy nodded. "Once again, you are so right."

"Hey, I'd better get going," Katie said. "I'm going to miss my ride."

"Would you save me a seat at the assembly tomorrow, if you get there before me? Sit in the front row, if there's room."

"Front row? Why? You want to be up close so you don't have far to run onto the stage when they call your name?"

"Something like that."

That evening Christy overheard her mom talking to Aunt Marti on the phone. "I tell you, she's a natural. I didn't even know it was my own daughter out there when she tried out. I'm so proud of her."

Christy listened quietly in the background as her mother went on about how wonderful everything was going for their family and how blessed and happy they were. Her final comment surprised Christy. "I have to admit, Marti, you and Bob were right about talking us into moving out here to California. Norm is content at Hollandale Dairy, David's reading has improved tremendously, and Christy, well, all I can say is, we are so proud of how she's turning out."

After Mom hung up, she began to fix dinner. Christy followed her into the kitchen.

"Mom," she began without really thinking through how to phrase her thoughts, "would you love me as much if I weren't a cheerleader? I mean, if I didn't get good grades or if I didn't make cheerleader, would you and Dad still be proud of me?"

"How can you even ask such a thing? You know we love you and are proud of you no matter what the circumstances."

"Yes, but I messed up on that whole prom thing."

"It worked out, Christy, and you learned from the situation. That's what matters."

"But what about cheerleading? I heard you talking to Aunt Marti about it and, well, what if I weren't a cheerleader?"

Mom leaned against the counter and put down the can of green beans she was about to open. A gentle look settled on her face. "Christy, all your father and I want is for you to become what God wants you to be. If that means becoming a cheerleader or a soccer player or president of the math club . . ."

Christy made a face. "Math club?"

"Okay, maybe not the math club. The point is, it doesn't matter to us. As long as you're obedient to what God wants you to be."

Those were intense words coming from Christy's mom. She had never before said anything like that. Especially the part about being obedient to God.

"Why do you ask, Christy?"

Christy almost told her mom all that was on her heart, but the right words didn't come.

"I don't know. I was just wondering," Christy said.

Mom sunk the can opener into the can of green beans and said, "Would you make the salad for me, please? There are two heads of lettuce in the refrigerator. Make sure you use up the littlest one first."

Christy pulled out the smaller head of lettuce and giggled to herself, remembering Katie's description of her corsage. Christy told her mom about it as they worked together, preparing dinner. They didn't have too many open, fun times like this, so it made tonight even more special. During moments like this, Christy felt more like an adult. It was as if the two of them were getting to be more on the same level and were becoming friends.

Christy thought of how much she liked these few times of open spaces in their relationship, when her mom would speak to Christy as though Christy were a friend, rather than a child. Christy wondered if her mother treasured these times, too.

The next morning Christy and her mom had another "becoming friends" moment when Mom offered to fix Christy's hair.

At first Christy said, "No, that's okay." Then she saw a look of disappointment on her mom's face and quickly said, "Well, okay, sure."

Inwardly, she figured if it didn't turn out, she could always change it at school. It had been years since her mother had "fixed" Christy's hair, and it seemed strange that she wanted to do it today.

Mom set to work and explained, "This is an old German farm girl's braid. I used to wear my hair like this all the time when I was your age."

Christy examined her hair in the mirror and said, "This is exactly what I saw in a magazine, and I couldn't figure out how to do it. I thought it was a brand-new style."

Mom laughed. "Funny how all the old styles come back around eventually."

Five minutes later Christy admired the results in the mirror.

Mom had begun a French braid right above Christy's ear and worked her hair into the braid so that it circled her head like a soft halo. The end tucked right behind her ear into the beginning of the circle. Christy carefully sprayed her hair, feeling thrilled with the way it had turned out and confident that she looked good.

"I'm coming to your assembly today," Mom said. "I'm only going to slip into the back, so you don't have to worry about looking for me or anything."

"That's okay, Mom. You don't have to come."

"I've worked everything out so I can be there. This is a big day for you, Christy. I'd like to be there to enjoy the moment of glory with you." Mom smiled into the mirror at her daughter. "I feel as if I've just placed a laurel wreath on your head."

"A what?" Christy returned the gaze, fastening tiny pearl earrings on her ears.

"Oh, I know I'm being silly. I was referring to ancient Greece at the Olympics when the winners received a crown made out of leaves as their reward."

"Oh. Guess we haven't come to that yet in our history class."

"I'll go see if David's ready," Mom said, looking cheery and pleased with life. "You need to leave in about five minutes." She began to walk away.

"Um, Mom?"

Mom turned and listened, her face looking soft and gentle— completely approachable.

"Mom, remember what you said last night about how I should obey God?"

"Yes."

"Well, I just want to say that if sometimes it seems that I've done something that doesn't make sense to anybody else, well . . .

maybe I've done the right thing, even if it seems weird."

Mom looked confused.

Christy tried to rephrase her statement. "I guess all I'm trying to say is that I want to obey God, and I want to do what He wants me to do and, well, I guess sometimes if I truly obey God, it will only make sense to me and not to other people. Does that make sense?"

"Sort of. Your heart is open to God, and that's what matters. Now get going. You don't want to be late."

Christy checked her appearance in the mirror and then knelt down and probed through a mound of dirty clothes in the back of her closet. Her hand touched the cold Folgers coffee tin, and Pooh toppled off his guard post.

"Hi, Pooh. Sorry I left you in there so long."

Christy placed Pooh on her bed and popped the lid off the coffee can.

"Christy," her mom called, "time to go."

"Coming."

Being careful not to crush any of the precious carnation buds, Christy fished through the dry petals and retrieved her "Forever" bracelet.

Then scooping up her books, she rushed out the front door and bounded down the steps under the jasmine trellis, ready for everything this bright spring day would hold.

CHAPTER THIRTEEN

Surprise!

The auditorium began to fill with students for the 2:00 assembly. Christy looked for Katie among the few people already sitting in the front rows, but she wasn't there. Slipping into the second row, Christy quietly waited.

Deep in her heart, she whispered a prayer. *Father God, I want to become the person You want me to be. I want You to be pleased with me. You are—*

Her prayer was interrupted by a familiar voice. "Hey, how's it going?"

"Todd? Todd!" Christy jumped up and impulsively gave him a hug. "What are you doing here?"

"Heard this was a big day for you." He looked excited, with his wide grin and clear eyes.

Suddenly aware that people were watching them, Christy motioned for Todd to sit next to her. He stretched his arm across the back of her chair and sat looking at her, still smiling. He clearly was proud of her.

"I like your hair," he said. "You look like an angel with a halo."

Christy felt thrilled and uncomfortable and confused all at the same time. "Thanks. But how did you know about the assembly today?"

"I was at your aunt and uncle's last night when Marti was talking to your mom. Thought I'd surprise you. Did I?" He looked almost silly, he was so pleased with himself.

"Yes! I still can't believe you're here. But, Todd, there's something I should tell you about the cheerleader announcement—"

This time Katie's voice interrupted her. "Christy! Todd?" Katie's face reflected her surprise. "Todd! Christy?"

"I know!" Christy laughed. "Kind of a surprise, huh? Do you want to sit by us?"

Katie inched her way into the empty seat on the other side of Christy as Todd pulled an envelope from his back pocket. "You want see my pictures from prom night?" he asked.

Christy's emotions plummeted. How could she say no? Especially with Katie leaning toward Todd and saying, "I want to see them. Pass 'em this way."

"Jasmine's mom took these at their apartment before the prom dinner." Todd lifted a photo out of the envelope as if it were a rare treasure and handed it to Katie.

Christy closed her eyes for an instant, then opened them and looked at the photo Katie now held in front of her. All of her jealousy fled. Christy's first thought sped to her lips, but she held back from speaking it. *That's Jasmine?*

The picture showed Todd standing tall and dashing in his tux with a teal blue bow tie and matching cummerbund. He looked finer than any knight in shining armor. Jasmine wore a long, blue satin gown with straight, long sleeves. The skirt covered the bottom part of her wheelchair, and in her lap lay one long-stemmed white rose with a blue ribbon.

Jasmine didn't have the long, flowing blond hair of a prom

queen, as Christy had imagined her having. Instead, Jasmine's dark hair was cropped short. Her hands lay useless in her lap, with fingers frozen in a twisted grip. And although she wore makeup, she still had a plain, simple-looking face.

But her smile! Her heart shone from her face as she smiled.

"Isn't she beautiful?" Todd asked.

Katie pulled her head back so Todd couldn't see her and gave Christy a doubtful look.

Christy knew exactly what Todd meant, so she sincerely answered, "Yes, she is. She's beautiful."

Jasmine deserved to have a special prom night, and she deserved to have it with Todd.

"So," Christy asked bravely, "did you have a good time at the prom?"

"We didn't go to the dance. Just out to dinner," Todd said. "I'm not big on dressing up and stuff like that. But I heard some of Jasmine's friends say they were all going to dinner in Laguna Beach before the prom. I thought taking Jasmine would be the best present I could give her—something no one else would think about giving. That's my favorite kind of gift."

Christy felt the cool metal of her "Forever" bracelet and realized how carefully Todd planned the gifts he gave. Her bracelet meant more to her at that moment than it ever had before. She was so glad she'd run back that morning and fished it from the coffee can.

"You didn't go to the prom, then?" Christy realized that neither she nor Rick nor Todd had gone. She had ridden a colossal emotional roller coaster for nothing. "You guys didn't go to the dance part of the prom?"

Todd looked at Christy as if he didn't understand her question. "No. Dances aren't exactly my idea of a good time."

"Tell me about it," Katie muttered.

"Jasmine and I had a great time with her friends at dinner, and that's the part that really mattered to both of us."

Christy remembered when she and Todd and the rest of her beach friends had gone ice-skating last Christmas, and Todd had turned out to be a klutz on the ice. She wondered if maybe he wasn't really comfortable with dances for some of the same co-ordination reasons. The thought made her smile. There were so many things she didn't know about Todd. She was glad things were back to normal so she could keep getting to know this one-of-a-kind guy.

Todd slipped Jasmine's treasured photo back into the envelope. "I can't wait for you to meet Jasmine," he told Christy. "I told her that you and I would fix breakfast on the beach for her one morning. Only this time the birds wouldn't get to the food. I told Jasmine her job would be to keep the seagulls away."

"You told her about our breakfast on the beach last Christmas?" Christy asked.

"Of course. She said she's anxious to meet you. You know, she asked if you were upset that I took her to the prom dinner instead of you, and I told her you weren't like other girls."

Christy felt awful. She was about to argue the point and tell Todd that she really failed more than succeeded, and that she'd worked herself into a jealous rage over his taking Jasmine to the prom, when the curtain began to go up in the noisy, packed auditorium.

A girl slid into the seat directly in front of Christy, then turned around and said, "Hi! Hope you didn't think I was going to miss this!" It was Teri.

"Hi," Christy greeted her and quickly introduced Todd.

The football coach began to introduce next year's lineup, and soon the stage bulged with proud young men roaring with school spirit and slapping each other on the back.

"And now," the coach bellowed into the microphone, "Kelley High's best all-around athlete from this year will introduce next year's cheerleaders! I present to you, Rick Doyle!"

Rick jogged onto the stage in his letterman's jacket, his half grin showing how much he loved the wild applause that filled the auditorium.

Will Rick see me sitting here with Todd? Will he even notice? Do I even care? Christy thought. Then she began to feel nervous. Up until then she had been fine. In the garden of her heart, she knew the right seeds had been planted, but now that the moment had come for everyone to see the harvest, she felt her stomach jumble. *What will everyone think of me? And do I even care?*

Rick stepped up to the microphone, seemingly quite at home in front of an audience, and waved his hands for the applause to die down. It reminded Christy of when Rick had announced her name as "Christina" in front of the youth group the first Sunday she visited his church with Katie.

That time he had embarrassed her and made her feel nervous to be noticed by him. Now she felt strong and unafraid of him. And not just because Todd was beside her. It was because she knew that she was becoming who she was meant to be, as her mom had said. And she could rest in that confidence. Not Rick nor anyone else could shake the strange confidence she felt in the midst of her nervousness.

"Okay! I have the list here," Rick said, holding up an envelope. "As I announce the cheerleaders by name, come on up and stand in front of these men that you're going to be cheering on to victory next fall."

Rick tore open the envelope and scanned the list before saying, "Renee Duvalt."

Renee sprang from her seat and with mock surprise, swished onto stage, giving Rick a perky little hug. With a halfhearted response to Renee, Rick kept looking at the list. Christy saw him turn it over and check the back.

Rick called the rest of the names loudly and clearly. Then he paused on the very last name.

Katie reached over, squeezed Christy's arm, and whispered, "Get ready! This is it!"

"And our final cheerleader is . . ." Rick paused for emphasis. "Teri Moreno!"

Christy felt as though the whole world were looking at her, gasping its surprise.

"Teri!" Katie snapped.

Teri turned around, stunned.

"But Christy . . ." she stammered.

"Go on, Teri! They called your name."

"But why?" Teri slowly rose from her chair, searching Christy's face for the answer.

Christy spoke clearly. "Because God wanted you to be a cheerleader, and I knew it."

Teri, dazed and overjoyed at the same time, gave Christy a big hug. Then she ran—leaped—onto the stage as the other girls whispered among themselves and clapped for her. She gave a mighty jump and eagerly received the astonished congratulations from the other girls. Then, facing the audience, Teri turned on her electric smile, shooting a current of absolute joy right at Christy.

Christy kept applauding until her hands hurt, ignoring Katie's nonstop questions.

Todd leaned over and said, "You did that, didn't you? You

gave up the spot you earned so she could be on the squad, didn't you?"

Christy nodded and blinked back the tears of happiness.

Rick's voice boomed over the microphone as he said, "I'd like to say something here. Please sit back down. I think it's important to say that some people give to our school in ways that no one else sees. Those people, and they know who they are . . ." Rick paused and looked directly at Christy. "Those people rarely get the thanks they deserve."

The auditorium had begun to quiet down.

"For those people who never quit giving of themselves, this is what I think of you." Rick crumbled the list and stuffed it into his pocket. Before a hushed audience, he slowly, dramatically, with deliberate strokes, stepped back and pounded the palms of his hands together in applause, his gaze glued on Christy.

Katie sprang to her feet and, facing Christy, joined in the applause. In a breath, the whole student body stood, clapping and cheering. Christy instinctively stood, too, surprised that the applause was for her.

Todd put his arm around her and spoke so she could hear above the roar, "They're clapping for you, Chris. They know a real God-lover when they see one." He leaned closer and added, "Or should I say, they know real love when they see it."

Christy felt the warmth of Todd's breath on her neck. She looked at him and said, "Are you sure?"

Todd laughed and held her tightly. "Am I sure? Just look up on the stage."

Christy saw the cheerleaders all lined up, smiling their approval at her and clapping. Even Renee, with a soft expression on her face, stood there clapping, clapping for Christy. Rick also stood there applauding, and looking like a guy who, indeed, was willing to wait.

And then Christy looked at Teri and knew for certain she'd made the right decision. Tears danced down Teri's cheeks as her dazzling smile filled the auditorium. Teri glowed—absolutely glowed. Just like an angel in the great forever.

Don't Miss These Captivating Stories in
THE CHRISTY MILLER SERIES

#1 • Summer Promise
Christy spends the summer at the beach with her wealthy aunt and uncle. Will she do something she'll later regret?

#2 • A Whisper and a Wish
Christy is convinced that dreams do come true when her family moves to California and the cutest guy in school shows an interest in her.

#3 • Yours Forever
Fifteen-year-old Christy does everything in her power to win Todd's attention.

#4 • Surprise Endings
Christy tries out for cheerleader, learns a classmate is out to get her, and schedules two dates for the same night.

#5 • Island Dreamer
It's an incredible tropical adventure when Christy celebrates her sixteenth birthday on Maui.

#6 • A Heart Full of Hope
A dazzling dream date, a wonderful job, a great car. And lots of freedom! Christy has it all. Or does she?

#7 • True Friends
Christy sets out with the ski club and discovers the group is thinking of doing something more than hitting the slopes.

#8 • Starry Night
Christy is torn between going to the Rose Bowl Parade with her friends or on a surprise vacation with her family.

#9 • Seventeen Wishes
Christy is off to summer camp—as a counselor for a cabin of wild fifth-grade girls.

#10 • A Time to Cherish
A surprise houseboat trip! Her senior year! Lots of friends! Life couldn't be better for Christy until . . .

#11 • Sweet Dreams
Christy's dreams become reality when Todd finally opens his heart to her. But her relationship with her best friend goes downhill fast when Katie starts dating Michael, and Christy has doubts about their relationship.

#12 • A Promise Is Forever
On a European trip with her friends, Christy finds it difficult to keep her mind off Todd. Will God bring them back together?

THE SIERRA JENSEN SERIES

If you've enjoyed reading about Christy Miller,
you'll love reading about Christy's friend Sierra Jensen.

#1 • Only You, Sierra
When her family moves to another state, Sierra dreads going to a new high school—until she meets Paul.

#2 • In Your Dreams
Just when events in Sierra's life start to look up—she even gets asked out on a date—Sierra runs into Paul.

#3 • Don't You Wish
Sierra is excited about visiting Christy Miller in California during Easter break. Unfortunately, her sister, Tawni, decides to go with her.

#4 • Close Your Eyes
Sierra experiences a sticky situation when Paul comes over for dinner and Randy shows up at the same time.

#5 • Without a Doubt
When handsome Drake reveals his interest in Sierra, life gets complicated.

#6 • With This Ring
Sierra couldn't be happier when she goes to Southern California to join Christy Miller and their friends for Doug and Tracy's wedding.

#7 • Open Your Heart
When Sierra's friend Christy Miller receives a scholarship from a university in Switzerland, she invites Sierra to go with her and Aunt Marti to visit the school.

#8 • Time Will Tell
After an exciting summer in Southern California and Switzerland, Sierra returns home to several unsettled relationships.

#9 • Now Picture This
When Sierra and Paul start corresponding, she imagines him as her boyfriend and soon begins neglecting her family and friends.

#10 • Hold on Tight
Sierra joins her brother and several friends on a road trip to Southern California to visit potential colleges.